UNFAIR MAGIC

BONNIE ELIZABETH

MY BIG FAT ORANGE CAT PUBLISHING

Unfair Magic
My Big Fat Orange Cat
Mystery 2021

My Big Fat Orange Cat Publishing
MyBigFatOrangeCat.com

ISBN: 978-1-953363-14-5 Trade Paperback
978-1-953363-15-2 Large Print Hardback

Murder marred my first time judging feline familiars at the local fair.

It's an honor to be considered for a judge position at the witch fair. It's an even greater honor to be chosen. For someone as young as I am, relatively speaking, it's almost unheard of. I'm not quite thirty and most of the judges had been on the fair circuit since I was a child. In fact, I watched my mom show in front of them in the casual feline class.

Local witch, LaDona Edwards had judged all three feline familiar classes and two of the ordinary classes since before I was born. She's a force of nature with long steel-gray hair that she keeps in a single braid that hangs down to her butt. She wears floral skirts with plenty of ruffles and still wears Birkenstocks with wool socks, though I have heard she uses spelled wool. She's kind of an anomaly not only for this era, but in rural Central Kentucky, though I expect she wouldn't raise an eyebrow someplace like Portland, Oregon.

At any rate, when she came to see me at the anniversary celebration of the opening of my cat cafe, I thought she was just making nice. But apparently, one of the working feline class judges was having back surgery and wouldn't be able to work at the local fair.

Many of the judges travel around to the various witch fairs that happen between April and October. Not all of them can make all the fairs so they pick locals to sit in on certain categories. If LaDona decided she liked me this time, I'd be on the rolls and whenever there was an opening on the panel for the working feline class, my name would come up.

Chances were, I'd never be able to leave and go to another fair, but just being part of the Waverton Fair was an honor I couldn't pass up.

Me, Jade Owlens, owner of Jade's Café, which has its own familiar feline room in the back, just like an ordinary cat café. I suppose the fact that I worked so closely with my familiar Mason, a big old ginger and white bi-color who rules the room with a velvet paw, was a big reason I'd been picked. The other was probably because I was used to having to work with people. I'd heard that the people showing can be intense and demanding.

Waverton's fair happens in mid-October and it's one of the latest witch fairs. I'm not sure how that happened. It's not as if Kentucky has great weather into October, particularly in Waverton. We're west of London, Kentucky and a bit south. The two-lane highway that takes you here wanders and curves through plenty of rolling hills. Because of that, we tend to be cooler than London or Lexington and summer is a popular time for people taking day trips to get out of the heat and humidity.

It's one reason I set the café up to appeal to ordinary people as well as witches. While most familiars, even those orphaned by the death of their witch, prefer to go to another witch, some like the idea of being part of an ordinary cat-loving home. They think of it as retirement.

Waverton itself isn't exactly an ordinary town any more than my cats are ordinary felines. We're the familiar capital of the United States and we're actually known around the world. We get quite the diverse set of witch tourists looking to do research at our specialty library or at the local university which caters to our specialization in familiars.

The library, of course, has a look-away spell on it for when ordinary folks come to visit. I'm not sure what they see, but whatever it is, it's far less interesting than the library is to a witch. Our fair is pretty much like that too. Ordinaries come in and see the ordinary tables and the familiars, which are all animals, and that's about it. They don't even consider going into the competition building due to spells. Anyone selling something in the fair booths that doesn't have an ordinary counterpart typically spells their booths to keep non-witches from noticing them.

The fair isn't long, just Wednesday through Sunday. I think the first two days are mostly for judging the crafts and foods. My sister, Julia is talented with cloth and sewing and she always enters. This year she entered an apron that she spelled to help people cook more flavorful foods. She also entered a quilt spelled to enhance er... romance in the bedroom, if you get my drift.

This meant that while I was bouncing around, excited by the whole fair idea, Julia was stressing out about winning. She works at a fabric store that also sells her crafted items. A win would get her a huge bonus because it would bring in more witches that would want to see her stuff and learn her spells.

Wednesday didn't require a lot from me as a judge. The working felines were showing on Saturday. It's another reason this was such an honor. Working class is a big class and those judges are typically well-known. Casual classes were on Wednesday, which were the least interesting because just about anyone could enter.

If there were less stressful competitions, casual classes were it, though I knew from when my mom entered, even that could be fraught. People take showing their familiars seriously.

Wandering around the fair, looking at who was selling what, I paused by my friend Trinity's table to chat with her. She worked at the specialty library and they always had a booth. This year it was towards the back of the big vendor building. The long, low building looked like a crappy warehouse from outside with metal sides and roof. It was so long that if I wore a Fitbit, which I don't, I'd definitely get my steps in each day. I'd left Mason home because I was mostly enjoying the sights. He'd join me for the pre-judging meetings with the other two working class judges, and then for the actual judging. Familiars have a role as important as their witches.

The library booth was next to the booth for the university and across from a couple of bookstore booths. The area smelled of old paper and the fresh sawdust that covered the dirt floor. I caught traces of burning from the chimney-shaped outdoor heaters that were spread around the space. Fans on the ceiling circulated the air. Given that there wasn't really any insulation, it was probably good that the fair wasn't earlier in the year. Far easier to heat than to try and cool it down.

While the fair wasn't all that busy yet, I noticed three or four people standing around the heaters, though it wasn't terribly cold inside. I had on a plain black turtleneck under a light fleece and I was almost too warm.

"Jade!" I turned to see Lyn Upton walking towards me.

Lyn and I had gone to school together, from kindergarten onward. She was more into athletics than I was so we didn't hang out the way I hung out with Trinity or even my other best friend, Natalie.

"What's going on?" I asked.

"I heard you're judging the working felines," Lyn smiled, a little too big and a little too eagerly. "I guess Medina and I will see you in the ring."

I noted the casual jeans and the red fleece she wore over a blouse that had the name of her pet sitting business on it. If I remembered correctly, she had a little place to keep pets on-site but she also did home visits. Medina, her familiar, probably worked with the on-site pets.

"I guess I will," I said.

"I don't know if you remember Medina. She's an Abyssinian. I got her before you opened the café, of course, or I'd have come in and visited there," Lyn paused as if waiting for an acknowledgment. Her blonde hair, tied back in a ponytail shook a bit as she waited.

I just smiled, not sure what to say.

"I just adore her, of course. And she's so good when I have skittish cats on-site. I'm sure you're aware of how helpful that can be, what with your familiar, Mason. I'm sure you'll find all sorts of things they have in common."

I smiled again and made a general sort of noise that I hoped was friendly. I had no idea what I was supposed to say.

Lyn gave me another smile and then led into, "How is the café business going?"

"Good," I said, which was true enough. I did feel good about my business. I noticed that Lyn's face looked a bit haggard and I wondered if married life hadn't agreed with her. I'd heard she and her husband were trying for kids, but it had been several years and they still didn't have any.

A few other people were talking loudly about the fair and their own familiars. Someone was looking for calming kennels and loudly demanded to know where he could find them. I didn't know so I didn't respond, but Lyn did and was eager to be helpful.

I took that moment to slip away from her, waving at Trinity, though I felt badly for just heading off. Still, the encounter with Lyn made me uncomfortable. Unfortunately, that wouldn't be my only uncomfortable encounter that day.

A few minutes later, having left the first vendor building, I entered the craft building. I could admire my sister's work there. This building was quieter, though it had the same metal walls and roof. No vendors sold items here and voices didn't carry as far thanks to all the quilts hanging from the ceiling. It still smelled like sawdust but also like cloth with a stray hint of lily.

From across the way, I heard one of the horses whinny. It made me want to giggle, so I knew that the horse familiar was particularly happy. Familiars come in all flavors, though I couldn't imagine having one as large as a horse. They were popular, of course, this being Kentucky.

I wandered through the quilts, looking at Julia's competition. I reached out to a few of them to see what sorts of spells were woven into them. I got snatches of tingling from the spells, but my sensations didn't actually tell what the spells did. I had to actually read the back of the little cards, something ordinaries would never think to do. Another spell, of course.

I was alone in the aisle I was walking down. The quilt in front of me was particularly striking. Someone had created a repeating pattern of applique horses. The spell on it was to increase the bond with a familiar, which was an interesting choice. The browns and golds of the fabric the horses were cut from contrasted nicely with the border in greens and golds. All in all, the quilt was quite striking.

A woman in a sweatshirt with an embroidered cat walked into the aisle from the other direction. She paused before the quilt while I was still admiring it, looking at the stitches, noting how finely done they were. Having a sister who quilts had taught me what to look for.

My cat-loving companion crossed her arms like she was some sort of quilt judge. Her lips turned down in a frown, particularly when she read about the spell on the back.

"I'm not sure a horse quilt would work with felines," she said, turning to me, her head held so high she could almost look down her nose at me. It was too bad she was shorter than I was.

She was a little older than me, too. She didn't smile when she spoke. It was clear she didn't like the quilt, although why she'd singled this one out to comment on, I didn't know. Maybe just having someone standing there to listen to her was all it took.

"The colors are nice, though," I said.

She sniffed a bit. I took a dislike to her, even though we should have had a bond given we were both cat lovers.

She looked more closely at the lanyard I wore around my neck that had my name and the fact that I was a judge on it. This would get me into places ordinary fair visitors wouldn't. It also meant I got a parking lot in the judge's lot behind the competition building. It wasn't a huge perk, but it was all gravel and if it started raining that would save my shoes.

"You're a judge?" the woman sounded incredulous.

I nodded.

"You look too young," she said. It was the same sort of implied criticism that she'd made about the quilt. "I can't believe LaDona would go for that."

I shrugged.

"I guess you'll see me in the ring," she said. "My familiar and I enter working felines." With that, she sniffed and strutted away.

A group of people came down the row talking. I heard a few oohs and ahhs over a couple of the quilts. I bit my lip, wondering if rude people were part and parcel of being a judge even when I wasn't in the ring. I hoped not. I wanted to be able to enjoy the fair and enjoy the honor of picking the finest working felines.

Lyn had already ruined by exploration of the first building and now I'd lost interest in the crafts. Fortunately, as I was leaving I ran into one of my best friends, Natalie. While normally that would have been an upswing on a particularly miserable day, this time it was more than fortunate.

2

Dressed in blue jeans and a red and white sweater, Natalie looked like a model. With her hair pulled back in a neat clip, Natalie clearly looked as if this was planned, a much more put together look than Lyn's slightly frayed and messy ponytail. Natalie couldn't look frayed if she tried. Her long legs, fair hair, and pale skin make her look like a Nordic goddess… next to whom I looked like a mousy servant.

My jeans never fit like hers, probably because my hips tend to be too wide. My hair is an ordinary brown though in the sun sometimes I get some reddish-gold highlights. Unfortunately, they never seem to last. Nor do I get much sun running an indoor business. I used to have them done in a salon when I got my hair cut but, lately, I've been hard-pressed to keep my hair trimmed into something resembling neatness.

Having a business that's going well and being honored as a judge was all well and good, but it did mean I was busy.

Natalie works in the hotel her family owns on the edge of Waverton. Her parents were home for a change, which meant she had a bit of time off while her parents took over management. Usually, Natalie stayed in charge. She loves it. Because it's an established business with more than a dozen employees, some of whom are shift managers, Natalie doesn't have to work quite the long hours I do even when her parents are gone, which is often.

At any rate, they were back for the fair and Natalie was able to take the afternoon off to wander around with me.

"Trinity said you snuck out of the other building when someone accosted you about the judging," Natalie said.

We were standing near the main front doors. I'd been thinking I'd be safer looking at horses and had intended to head to the horse barn across the way. The smell of horses and cows and the manure that goes with the larger animals hit my nose as I stood there, but it wasn't an unfamiliar stink. The hills surrounding Waverton were home to many farms.

"It seems like everyone has something to say. Lyn Upton was being nice like she wanted me to remember her. The woman I met in here was just rude," I said.

Natalie shrugged. "I haven't seen Julia's entries yet," she said, not caring that I felt harassed already.

With Natalie around, I probably wouldn't get so much unwelcome attention. With her striking looks, I tended to blend into the background. In high school, I had often felt a bit jealous, but in this case, I was just as pleased to let that happen.

I followed Natalie as she walked past some of the glass cases holding the smaller craft items. Baby booties and scarves. I noted a few gloves and mittens as well. While they were all nice things and I noted the creative spells on the cards, I didn't have the eye to decide which of these were nicer than another.

Just beyond were the quilts, the large ones hanging from the ceiling. The baby quilts were under glass like the other small items. I wasn't certain a baby quilt was small enough to walk away with, but I guess you never knew.

There were three aisles of quilts and Natalie and I talked about which ones we particularly loved.

"I do like that yellow and green sampler quilt," Natalie said pointing to the one on the end.

I noted that the quilter was still a teenager, which impressed me. I knew from Julia that the tiny stitches were finely done. The points of the triangles were sharp. All in all, it was a fine quilt. The spell was a calming one, which is common enough for blankets. I had a feeling that while the quilting was well done, the lack of creativity in the spells would grade the maker down.

"I can't believe Luanne Duncan," a woman said from behind us. "She thinks she and that cat are going to take the overall working group. Like cats win working groups."

I glanced behind me. Both women were closer to my mother's age than mine. One had very red hair but it was clearly not a natural red. Her red didn't exist except in a bottle. The other was stocky and gray-haired. Both were in jeans.

The red-haired woman who had been speaking was standing upright, hands clasped close to her sides, almost as if she was afraid her stomach would fall out of her loose shirt. The other woman stood slightly stooped and her face was pinched in. She looked worried.

Seeing me looking at them, the red-haired woman gave me a smile and a wave. Maybe it was the red lanyard that identified me as a judge.

"She won't win all class. Dogs always do and your Kandy Karmen will place, I know it," the stooped woman said.

The red-haired woman shushed her. The older woman looked around, saw Natalie and me, and smiled.

"Just dog talk, of course," she said.

I gave a tight smile and Natalie and I walked down the aisle the other way. I heard the two women whispering, but I had no idea what they were talking about.

"See, they didn't try to make nice to you," Natalie said.

"They have dogs," I said. "I judge the working felines. I don't get to judge the overall group. I don't have the seniority."

Natalie shrugged. We continued down the next aisle. Julia's quilt was displayed there and I paused in front of it. She'd done a close-up of two cats looking at a mouse. She'd used primarily batik fabrics to create the scene. The eyes of each cat seemed to shimmer in the light. She called it "Concentration" and the spell she'd used was to help someone concentrate, of course.

"She's really good," Natalie said.

I had to admit I thought it was one of the best quilts in the show. I might have been biased, though. The watercolor quilt across the aisle of an iris in a pond was equally eye-catching.

"I love this quilt," I said, looking back at Julia's. "Of course, she used Mason for the cat with the greenish-gold eyes on the right. She matched fabrics up against him for probably fifteen minutes. Mason can't imagine another quilt being better."

"Of course he can't," Natalie smiled. Natalie's familiar, LaRue would no doubt have said the same thing. All cats had a certain level of pride in common.

"I wish I could do that," a familiar voice said, though I hadn't ever heard the longing in it before. I looked back and there was Flori. Flori had come into my shop last summer. I hadn't known it at the time, but she was under a spell to give her magic. Since then, she'd been living with a witch to learn how to use her talents.

A short, stocky woman came up behind her, her eyes brilliant blue. "It is wonderful. But it takes practice."

Flori shrugged. Her thick dark hair that used to swirl messily about her shoulders, completely untamed, was now harnessed in a large gold barrette. "I tried using needlework to focus, but it was all so ugly."

"Practice," the woman said again, smiling indulgently at Flori.

Flori made a face and then met my eyes. I noted the slight widening as she recognized me.

"You're the café lady," she said. Then she looked at my lanyard. "And a judge?"

I nodded. "It's good to see you here, Flori."

Flori laughed a little. "My parents let me go stay with a cousin they don't have, but think they do. Apparently, they were tired of my shenanigans."

Flori's comment would only make sense to a witch who knew her background. I inferred from it that the WBI had spelled her parents to believe they had a cousin so that Flori could go live with a witch trained in helping young witches learn to handle their powers.

"Are you living in Waverton?" I asked. It was probably the best place for her. Having come into magic so late in life she was likely to make more mistakes than children who come more slowly into their magic and are raised to understand that they can't show off what they are.

"Just on the outskirts. I'm Nadine." The older woman with Flori reached out her hand. I took it, feeling the strength in her shake.

"Nadine used to have a daycare because she's really good with kids but she decided it was too much work," Flori said with barely enough time to take a breath. "We're talking about maybe getting me a familiar soon because they can help me manage my magic. I told her I wanted a cat. I feel safe with cats."

"And you run the café," Nadine smiled. "I thought an adult cat would be good for her, but I know that she didn't exactly put her best foot forward. I've talked to a few breeders to see if they're petting out any of their stock. A Maine Coon would be good. Solid and easy-going."

I'd worked with breeders enough to understand Nadine's terminology of petting out, which meant sending an adult queen or stud to be adopted as a pet rather than a show cat or part of furthering the breeding line.

"Or a Ragdoll," Natalie said. "They're easy, too."

"Calm," Nadine said, "But not as sure and solid as a Maine Coon, I don't think. If you get a cat with that sort of personality, let me know."

"I will," I said. "And Flori is welcome to come and visit and see if she bonds with any cats there. I don't think I currently have any felines that are that calm, but you never know."

Some familiars were better at absorbing excess magic and grounding it than others. Chances were, because she wasn't used to having magic, Flori was bleeding it all over. I was glad she had someone like Nadine to take her in hand.

"Nadine has goats," Flori said. She giggled. "I never thought I'd like goats, but they're fun."

I couldn't exactly imagine Flori with a goat, but that didn't mean she couldn't enjoy them just for the animals they were.

Nadine smiled at Natalie and me and led Flori off.

"That was interesting," Natalie said.

I had to agree. Flori was much easier going, more like a young teenager than the entitled brat she'd been when she'd first come into my café. Of course, she'd been terrified then and didn't even know enough to understand why.

I was still musing on that when I heard a scream. Natalie and I barely glanced at each other before we both hurried out of the aisle to head further into the building. Unfortunately, between the quilts and the other cubical walls to showcase artwork, we couldn't just look down the room to see where the scream had come from.

Instead, we had to work our way back, looking down each aisle. I noticed a small crowd when we got to an aisle filled with photography. Lying in front of a black and white image of a horse and a dog touching noses, lay the critical woman I'd talked to just before I'd run into Natalie.

Her eyes bulged and her mouth was open, her tongue thick. Someone was trying to pull off a scarf that had wrapped itself around her neck. It looked similar to scarves that I'd seen earlier in the judging cases. Nothing had been missing when Natalie and I walked by, though.

I felt an icy tingle running up my arms and I knew there was negative magic attached. Natalie already had her phone and was calling the Witch's Bureau of Investigation. We were going to need someone to untangle the magic and hopefully save the woman on the floor, though I had a feeling it was already too late for her.

3

From the looks of the woman, I guessed someone had strangled her. With the feel of dark magic, I wondered if it came from the scarf. She hadn't been wearing it when I saw her earlier. I backed up a bit, the scene making my stomach feel a bit funny.

I listened vaguely to the conversations around me, all of them shocked. The usual comments of having just seen her or talked to her. I realized that had been my first thought, too.

"Do you know her?" Natalie whispered.

I shook my head. "I saw her in the aisle by the horse quilt. She didn't like it much." Maybe the person who made the horse quilt had overhead and hadn't like the comments? Of course, that seemed like a lot to go through for someone like that.

A woman with short blonde hair streaked with green turned and looked at me. She was older than I thought, though she wasn't old. Her heavy arms and the lines around her eyes suggested she was at least forty. I'd have placed her at about twenty when I first noticed her. The jeans she wore were low around her hips and the bright lime long-sleeved Henley t-shirt both made her seem younger.

"Really? You're a judge," the blonde said.

"I haven't judged anything yet," I said. "I talked to her a bit in another quilt aisle, though." Just in case this person decided to be a busy body and insist I said I had never seen the woman, when in fact I just didn't know who she was.

"Yeah, but she was favored to win the working feline class," Blondie said. She looked at me up and down, daring me to deny that.

I knew that every year there were favorites to win. From what I understood the favorites were those who worked hard with their familiars. I couldn't fault that. But when LaDona had come to me to ask me to be a judge, I had worked to not pay attention to who people liked. I didn't want to let that influence my decisions in the ring.

"As a judge, I've worked to avoid that sort of conversation," I said, hoping that would keep Blondie from making judgments.

The woman gave a hmmph and turned away as if she didn't believe me. It was true, though.

Natalie touch my shoulder and pulled me back deeper into the crowd. "Don't let her get to you. She's right, though. I think the dead woman was entered in the working feline class. She was talking to one of the desk people when I was on last night. She and her cat are animal communicators for ordinaries."

Interesting use of the powers and probably slightly unethical. However, if she let it be known and the WBI hadn't investigated and charged her, far be it from me to decide she was in the wrong.

"She was in the aisle with me just before I ran into you. She was the woman who was so critical of the horse quilt. You don't suppose someone got angry about that, do you?" I asked. As I said it aloud, I realized how foolish that sounded. I mean, even if some random person disliked the quilt, it wouldn't make a difference. Craft judges didn't have special badges, but she didn't talk like someone who knew about crafts, just what she liked and didn't like.

My sister would have gone on about the stitching and the quality of the materials and creativity before criticizing it for perhaps being too familiar specific for the spell the creator had put on it.

Of course, if the dead woman was that critical about everything, maybe she'd said the wrong thing to the wrong person.

"Really?" Natalie asked. "Who would get that angry about someone making critical comments to a random stranger? It's not like you're a craft judge."

I nodded. "She did seem like nothing made her very happy. Maybe she said the wrong thing to the wrong person. I mean, if I had made that quilt, maybe I'd get mad that she didn't see all the work I put into it."

Natalie made a face and shook her head. "Enough to kill someone?"

I shrugged. I doubted I'd kill someone for any reason, other than to save my life, but someone else might feel differently.

The WBI arrived before I could say anything more, pushing people aside so I knocked into a tiny dark-haired woman behind me nearly knocking her over. The whispers quieted.

The feel of dark magic still tingled along my arms. A WBI agent took a long sniff and then made some hand movements. The tingling in my arms calmed. A spell to clear the negativity. Another agent pulled the scarf off the dead woman and another began a spell, perhaps to see if they could pick up echoes of what had happened.

I stepped back, both because I wanted to and because the crowd that had gathered was being pushed back by the WBI. Tom Alsez was one of the local officers working on crowd control. Tom and my sister were dating and it seemed like they might be fairly serious. He's a good guy and I was glad to see him there. I noted the way he looked at everyone in the crowd. He'd put a memory spell on to remember who he noticed in the crowd.

The scarf had to be the instrument of death. I remembered someone kneeling beside the woman trying to pull the scarf off but having a difficult time. Originally, I had thought they were just rather panicked but thinking back, the spell must have prevented them from removing it.

Most people don't carry around scarves infused with negative magic. It takes power to use magic that way. I mean anyone can do small negative spells and kids learn a few of them when they're growing up. It's one thing that makes someone like Flori so dangerous. She hadn't learned the consequences of negative spells.

A common kid spell considered negative allowed the witch to poke someone from afar. It was more annoying than evil. But because the intent was to cause irritation or harm, witches considered the spell negative. Any spell meant to cause harm typically drained the user of energy faster.

That meant that a student using the spell to poke another student a few times would probably have a hard time staying awake by the end of the day. Usually, the school figured out who had been casting the spell by who couldn't keep their eyes open. Unless, of course, the caster had gotten smart enough to cast it towards the end of the school day anyway.

Last period tended to be a bit wilder when it came to spells. All kids tended to pick up on how to avoid getting caught pretty quickly.

But even then we learned that it wasn't always easy to

avoid notice. Witch parents took notice of unusual sleepiness. Not everyone felt negative magic like I did, but other people smelled it. Some witches could even see it.

I glanced around at the people in the group, wondering if anyone looked particularly tired. However, everyone appeared to be wide awake. Of course, most of us were having an adrenaline rush from finding someone who'd just been strangled.

Medics rushed in, pushing us in another direction. Natalie took my hand and started pulling me away from the crowd. More people had arrived, probably attracted to the commotion. Bodies pressed against me squishing me between Natalie and a woman wearing too much floral perfume.

"Do you think she'll be okay?" I whispered to Nat as we slipped towards the far door. A few people were coming in, but they were mostly hoping to look through the building, not to see what was happening. Of course, people being people, several headed towards the crowd, wanting to find out what was going on. Others avoided the crowd, turning and heading the other way.

"Would you be okay looking like that?" Natalie asked, glancing at me. "I mean, her tongue was thick and she looked sort of blue. I can't imagine that she wasn't dead."

"But the medics…" I started.

"They have to call. Have to try," Natalie reminded me. "But maybe she wasn't quite dead and immediate attention will help, but I don't think so. Not the way the magic smelled."

Natalie only smelled particularly strong magic, which meant this was a major spell.

"Do you think someone made that scarf for her on purpose?" I asked. "I wonder who gave it to her. She didn't have it when I talked to her and that was just before you arrived."

"Maybe fifteen minutes, then," Natalie said. "You'll need to tell Tom. I saw him working the crowd. He'll be coming around to question us because we were there."

I nodded, drawing in a few deep breaths.

"Or you can just tell me," a red-haired woman said. Her face was all angles and sharp edges, her eyes hawk-like. Her auburn hair, clearly natural, or colored to look as natural as possible, was her best feature. She was dressed in a black pantsuit and wore a WBI badge that said her name was Lina and nothing else. That was more information than the WBI normally gave out.

Natalie and I exchanged a look. I had met Lina before. In fact, she'd helped with the investigation into what had happened with Flori. She hadn't been particularly nice at that time and from the hardness in her eyes, I doubted she'd be any nicer this time.

"This is, after all, the second time you've apparently had information about a murder," Lina continued, holding the badge. She wasn't going to let me leave without talking to her.

4

I was starting to feel a bit like one of the characters in the amateur detective mysteries my mom likes to read and is always sharing the plots with me. I mean, Lina was right. This was the second time I'd been on the periphery of a murder. But this time I really was just on the periphery, unlike last time when my shop had been targeted.

"I don't know much," I said. "I saw the woman or at least someone who looked kind of like her in the same sweatshirt, about fifteen or twenty minutes ago when I was looking at the quilts."

"Did you also see her?" Lina asked Natalie.

"I came later," Natalie said. She didn't volunteer how we had come to be together and I reminded myself not to say too much. Tyson, my boyfriend—something that still gave me a thrill to think—talked about how people never helped themselves telling the police too much.

"Were you two planning to meet up here?" Lina asked.

"We were supposed to meet up by the specialty library," I said. "But one of the witches entering the working feline class was there and was acting oddly."

Lina raised an eyebrow.

"I'm a judge," I said, showing off my badge rather like Lina had shown off hers. "I think she was being extra nice so I'd be more inclined to think well of her in the ring. Instead, it seemed a little creepy. I slipped out of the vendor building and came over here. Natalie showed up a few minutes later."

"Did you talk to the vic?" Lina asked.

"She talked to me," I said. "She commented on a quilt I was looking at. The one with the horses that has the spell to increase the bond with the familiar. She thought it was awfully horse specific and thought it should have had a more inclusive theme."

Lina nodded. "And what did you say?"

"That I thought the quilt was pretty." I looked down, feeling stupid. I mean I hadn't even had a good comment, just that I liked it.

"And then what?" Lina made a note on a pad. I knew she had a magical recorder, but I suppose it helped her to write things down anyway. Either that or she thought it looked more intimidating.

"She went down the aisle one way and I went the other. She hadn't been very nice. She noted that I was a judge and questioned whether LaDona had really asked me." I wasn't telling the story very well. "And it made me feel weird and I just wanted to get back to my friends, so I started to leave and found Natalie."

Tyson would still hate how much I had talked. And to the WBI. But it couldn't be helped. Besides, I wouldn't know where to start to do a spell on a scarf to strangle someone.

Lina looked up and stared at me for a few moments. My heart pounded. I was certain she thought there was more, like maybe while talking I had had time to knit a scarf and set a negative magic spell. Maybe she was waiting for me to collapse in negative magic fatigue, though if I were a regular practitioner of that sort of magic, I'd probably be okay. It was as if the body got used to such things after a time. Kind of like running, which is something else I've never quite gotten used to.

"Nothing else?" Lina asked.

"Natalie and I were wandering back through the quilts when we heard the scream and we went to find out what was happening. By the time we got there, there were already people around, people calling for help, and the woman was on the ground with the scarf..." I couldn't finish. The image of her was imprinted on my mind and I had no desire to bring the image back up into the forefront of my imagination.

Lina looked over at Natalie. "I just saw her when she was down. She was pretty obvious with a cat sweatshirt, so I think Jade recognized her from that. And she said that the dead woman hadn't worn a scarf when she saw her."

Mentally, I thanked Natalie. That would explain why I was so certain about who it was on the ground. It wasn't like I'd seen the woman with her tongue hanging out before.

"You said someone else came up to you and talked to you about judging?" Lina asked, looking down at her notes. I doubted she really needed her notes but it probably made her look more serious.

"Yeah. Lyn Upton. She's local. I knew her from school, sort of. We were friends but not super close. Anyway, she went on about me being a judge and made it sound like I should favor her because I knew her," I said.

"Do you think she could have been the one to murder this woman?"

"Lyn?" I repeated. I felt my eyes get wide. It was the last thing I could imagine, although I wasn't surprised that Lina's mind went there.

Lina waited, not saying anything. If there was one thing I

had learned about the WBI in my brief exposure to them, it was that they were good at standing there and staring at me, waiting for me to say something. I should have remembered that when I was being questioned.

"I can't imagine it," I said. "She's a friend. She's nice. I mean, I don't talk to her tons, and so I suppose anything is possible, but it seemed like she was just trying to ingratiate herself in hopes that I might be nicer to her. I don't know. It didn't seem like she was desperate."

Natalie patted my shoulder.

Lina nodded. "Your sister does fabric art, doesn't she?"

I nodded, frowning.

"She do the horse quilt?"

I shook my head. "She did the batik close-up of two cats and a mouse..." My eyes widened as I remembered the conversation the women with the dogs had.

"What?" Lina demanded watching my face.

"There were two women. I think one entered the working dog class. They were talking about someone named Luanne and her cat winning the overall working class and they thought that dogs ought to take it."

"So you think they could have done it?" Lina asked.

"I don't know," I said. "I mean, they were talking. And it sounds like everyone in the working class thought this Luanne was the person to beat but I don't even know if the dead woman was named Luanne."

Lina gave a quick nod and closed her tablet. She didn't say a word as she turned to leave. I suppose the fact that I wasn't told not to leave town was good. Of course, with the WBI, they could pretty much track me anywhere if they really wanted to. Not that I was planning to leave town or anything.

"Come on," Natalie said. "Let's go tell Trinity what's going on."

I let her pull me outside onto the dirt path. Only one other person was out there and they were walking from the food building back into the quilt and craft building. Natalie led me out towards the main path, a wide area of dirt. A big wagon of hay and scarecrows sat in the middle and families crowded around, ready to snap some photos.

I heard laughter, which seemed inappropriate after what had happened, but most of the people at the fair didn't know what had happened just yet. A goat bleated over the low conversations.

We made our way down the dirt lane to the vendor building so we could talk to Trinity. I had a feeling I'd be getting fewer comments from potential entrants now that Natalie was with me. Natalie spoke her mind much more freely than I did. I pitied anyone who tried to get on my good side with her there.

The vendors were busier now. A big bald man walked past us holding a large popcorn, which smelled heavenly. My stomach growled. Breakfast had been quite a while ago and had consisted mostly of coffee. I couldn't believe that I was hungry after what I'd seen. While my body clearly decided it needed more fuel, my brain was less ecstatic about eating.

With that internal conflict, I followed Natalie through the vendor booths towards the specialty library's booth. Fortunately, we were tracing a path I had already taken so I didn't feel I was missing anything as I passed the booths for calming carriers and collars that tracked a pet's movements. While both those things were theoretically possible for ordinary folks, ours were done with magic and were much more reliable.

I paused by a booth that had books on familiar breeds and eyed them while Natalie and I waited for a crowd to disperse in front of Trinity's booth. Trinity was smiling at everyone, but I could see faint traces of strain in that smile. She was already tired. The crowd seemed to have a ton of questions and I wondered if this was what a typical day was like in the library.

"You judge working breeds?" a man looking at the books asked me, leaning around to stare at my lanyard.

"Felines," I said.

He nodded. He was tall and broad with a nose like a beak. "I judged for a couple of years. Not here, of course. I don't know familiars well. But I judged up in Oregon. We do herbs there and I was good with potions. It's amazing how people react when they know you're a judge. Sometimes I think we let too much ride on what awards witches have gotten before we use their services."

I gave him a tight smile.

"This year someone died," the young man behind the booth with the books said. He looked too young to be manning the booth by himself, his eyes big behind wire-framed glasses. His t-shirt looked a size too large and his jeans were about an inch too short, showing off the tops of his tennis shoes and a portion of white sock hugging skinny ankles.

I wondered how he had gotten the job of sitting there. His reedy voice and ill-fitting clothing didn't inspire confidence.

"Jared," a woman said. She looked old enough to be his mother. She had two large cups of soda and she handed one off to Jared. Unsurprisingly, he took it gratefully.

"Sorry. I tell him not to gossip but he can't get his mind around that sometimes," she said. "Can I help you with a book?"

"Just looking," I said. The tall man who had once judged had disappeared while I'd been paying attention to Jared.

"I was just telling them that someone died," Jared said to his mom. "It's not gossip. It's true! You heard everyone talking about it!"

I couldn't help but smile at his defense. The crowd moved along and there was a short break, so I slipped over to the specialty library booth leaving Jared to his mother's wrath.

Trinity was already talking to Natalie. Natalie looked disappointed and Trinity looked serious, her soft features hardened into something almost sad-looking.

"I heard what happened," Trinity said to me. "You talked to this woman?"

I nodded.

"I heard she wasn't very nice," Trinity went on. "In fact, rumors are flying. Did you know that someone said she cheated in last year's competition and they weren't sure they were even going to let her enter this year?"

I hadn't heard that. I wondered if someone else was sure this woman was cheating and had decided to take matters into their own hands. I tried to remind myself that it wasn't my job to figure out what was going on, but I couldn't help being curious.

Trinity and Natalie and I talked a bit more. Several groups came by, talking and laughing. Nat and I stepped aside to let Trinity talk. We were fine until I felt a touch on my arm.

LaDona had walked up, I would say silently except she could have been banging a drum and I'm not sure I would have heard with all the conversations around and the music playing from various booths.

"LaDona!" I said, surprised. I wondered what she wanted.

"One of your entrants has died," LaDona said. "It's no secret that she was favored to win. She and her familiar worked incredibly well together and practiced not only in her work, but went through the common challenges daily."

I nodded. "It's terribly sad."

"More than that, I've heard she was probably murdered. I don't need to tell you that it won't look good for your judging if you reward a murderer by letting them place," LaDona said staring at me.

My jaw dropped just a bit. I couldn't believe she just expected me to know who had murdered this woman.

LaDona turned and left. I glared after her, fuming. Suddenly, it was my job, or at least my potential judging reputation, to find out who had murdered the witch.

5

When LaDona disappeared into the crowd, I looked over at Natalie. She had been talking to a teenage girl who was giggling. I didn't recognize her. No doubt she was staying at the hotel. Plenty of people came to Waverton just for the fair and those who reserved first always ended up staying at Natalie's hotel.

Waverton had a few bed and breakfasts, but they weren't terribly convenient for those with large animal familiars. Most witches coming to Waverton took their familiars with them, particularly for the fair. If they couldn't stay here, they had to stay outside of town. There were several hotels just off the freeway which was about half an hour away. Not an impossible drive, but those in the know preferred to stay at Natalie's.

It surprised me that no one had ever set up another hotel in town. Natalie said her folks had even looked into building a second hotel on the other side of town, but just hadn't gotten around to it. It would be completely possible. She'd heard through the hotel grapevine that a chain hotel was thinking about an area on the highway up to Louisville, but it hadn't made a commitment on the land it was considering.

Natalie finished her conversation and the girl turned, her brown hair disappearing into a group of three people who walked by. I got a whiff of coffee which made me smile a little.

"Did you hear what LaDona said?" I whispered to Natalie.

She hadn't, of course, having been engrossed in conversation with the teenager, so I told her.

"It's like she expects me to somehow know who killed this woman!" I said.

"I guess we'll just have to find out, then," Natalie said. Most friends would have offered their sympathy for my position and given me room to rant about how unfair it was. Natalie was a fixer and this was her way of fixing the problem. I looked at the specialty library's booth where Trinity was now talking to three older men, all dressed in baggy jeans and worn sweatshirts. They looked so much alike with their white hair and protruding chins that I wondered if they were brothers.

Given that they all seemed to be asking questions before Trinity even finished speaking, I wasn't going to get any comfort from her for quite some time.

Natalie waved over in Trinity's direction, so I did too. I let Natalie lead me out of the vendor building and into the outside air. Clouds were drifting in, but so far they all look white and fluffy and not at all threatening. I had heard rain was in the forecast, but not for today.

"So, we think her name was Luanne, right?" Natalie said, quietly as we walked up towards the food dome. The food dome was basically a huge dome with the typical fair food vendors. If it was greasy, messy, and not good for you, the fair offered it. Popcorn was sold from several carts placed around the grounds, one near the entry, one close to the dome, and, I knew for a fact, one on the midway, which was just on the other side of the food dome in a section all its own.

People brushed past us or sauntered along behind us. I was kind of surprised at how busy it was. I normally didn't visit the fair on Wednesday and would have thought fewer people could make it out. However, I remembered my mom going on Wednesday because she had to judge and there were a lot of witches who enjoyed checking out the crafts and foods on the first day to determine what they liked before the judges awarded the ribbons.

In addition to those folks, there would always be witches who wanted to see certain competitions, particularly if family or friends were entered. And, like my mom, others thought that a Wednesday would be less crowded, though I had yet to see a fair day not filled with people.

"I guess so. I mean the dog people were talking about someone named Luanne and her cat." I frowned. I had no way of knowing if those folks had actually been talking about the woman who had died. I wasn't sure why Natalie seemed sure they were.

"Maybe you should call Tyson and let him know what's going on," Natalie said. "He'd have reason to check in with the police about the victim and we could get information that way."

"Or I could ask Julia," I said. "She's dating Tom and I'll probably be talking to him soon enough about what I saw or didn't see. Unless Lina lets him know she talked to me. Not that the WBI is very good about sharing information with anyone."

Natalie made a face, but gave a nod, agreeing with me. The WBI witches were unpredictable. The father of one of my employees worked in cybercrimes for the WBI so I tried not to generalize too much, but it was difficult not to. My only encounter with them had been when Trinity was being investigated for murdering her boss and it hadn't been good.

In fact, if anything, Lina had been nicer than she had been when I knew her as Red. I wondered if she'd been outed because she'd been in town before and so had to use a real name while patrolling the fair. Or maybe Lina wasn't really her name either, though I had no idea why the WBI insisted upon fake names.

"Julia might get some gossip out of him," Natalie said. "I think you should do both."

"And what are you going to do?" I asked.

"First, I'm going to have lunch and then I'll go back to the hotel and check our registers. I want to know if we have a Luanne checked in and, if so, if she has a familiar. I can get some basic background on her by doing a few searches."

"Trinity can help. And she's dating Tyson's new investigator so I bet he can help, too," I said. Trinity had always been good at research. She worked in a library, after all. And if she asked for help, I was willing to bet investigators had access to places on the internet that most people didn't have. Places that would tell us about Luanne's background and any run-ins with the police, not that any problems with the WBI would show up.

Natalie gave me a long look before nodding.

"What?" I asked.

"I'm just not sure about Liam," she said speaking of the new investigator.

"Why not?" I followed her towards the food court.

Natalie sighed. I realized that Liam had immediately connected with Trinity and had hardly noticed Natalie. That wasn't a common happening. Naturally, Natalie would distrust someone who hadn't at least noticed her charms.

"I think he's a little full of himself," she finally said. "And he's a bit cagey. I realize some of that is because he investigates for a law firm, but there's something about the way he doesn't talk about himself. And I know he wants to move to Chicago someday, although why, I don't know. Considering the size of the city, there aren't many witches there and the traffic is horrible, not to mention the weather."

I shrugged. "Chicago is off in the future. If he really fell in love with Trinity, I bet he'd change his mind. At worst, he might go off to Louisville."

We paused by the dome. The large rounded white building almost glowed despite the slightly overcast sky. The clouds were darker than they had been, but hopefully, the rain would hold off. I breathed in the smells of hot dogs, fries, and cinnamon. My stomach growled again.

"Noodles?" Natalie asked, heading inside before I answered.

It would be easy enough for me to go to a different booth once inside, but Natalie didn't wait for me to make a different decision. Not that it mattered. I loved the noodles. They were sort of like a particularly greasy version of yakisoba and they were one of my go-to fair foods. That and the big burritos they made at the booth next door.

I followed Natalie to the line at the noodle place. Fortunately, the dome wasn't that crowded. It was a little past noon and people wandered but not too many were waiting for lunch. I hadn't seen a lot of people sitting down to eat in the big tent off to the side, either. That would change in the coming days.

After getting our food, Natalie and I found a place to sit and went back to talking about the murder.

"It seems like LaDona thought that was Luanne," I said. "So maybe there are people who know the dead woman. I mean, just because we're not sure..."

"After lunch, let's go into the competition building," Natalie said, clearly forgetting that she had planned to go back to the hotel and sleuth there. "Casual felines and canines are being shown this afternoon. People will be gossiping about a murder even if it's not in that class. We can listen in. We can also listen to what others think happened."

I slurped up some noodles so I couldn't agree right away, though Natalie didn't care. She'd already decided that was what we were doing. So long as she didn't stand over me to call Tyson and let him know I had talked to the WBI without an attorney, that was fine. Not that he'd be mad, but I had a feeling I'd be getting a lecture.

I sipped at the sweet tea I'd gotten, waiting for Natalie to finish. She eats more slowly than I do even when she's eager to start another adventure.

"Jade!" I turned at the sound of my sister's voice.

Julia stood behind me with her friend Ashley. Both of them wore their dark hair trimmed short so that it framed their faces. In some ways, I thought Julia looked more like Ashley than she did me. I admired the quilted front of her sweatshirt jacket and noted that Ashley had a similar one, though Julia's was red and Ashley's was gray.

"Hey you," I said, scooting over on the bench. Julia had a smoothie of some sort. Another thing I'd be getting one of the days I was there, though I found them to be more of a snack food than a meal.

"Did you hear about what happened in the craft building?" Julia asked, scooting in. Ashley sat beside her rather than going across the way to sit beside Natalie. Ashley had never liked Natalie and I wasn't quite sure why, though if I had to guess it was because they were too much alike and two bosses don't always work well together.

"I was there," I said. "I mean, not right there, but Natalie and I heard the scream."

"Wow!" Ashley said, peering around Julia. "How awful. It's

bad enough that I had a scarf in the competition and we've all been told to come in for questioning."

"It wasn't her scarf," Julia said. "Tom described it as purple and blue and the spell was negative. You know Ashley can't handle things like that."

"And purple is not my color," Ashley said.

"Do you know who it was?" I asked. "I saw her, sort of, but don't know her name."

"She would have been in your competition," Julia said. "Luanne Duncan."

"She did crafts as a hobby," Ashley filled in. "And I heard she wanted to judge crafts, but she did one year at a more local fair and was never asked back. I guess she was pretty hard-nosed about it."

I filed that away.

"It's so weird, though, that someone killed her like that," Julia went on. "You'd need a scarf that you knew didn't have magic lingering or that could set things off. Even ordinaries who do needlecrafts can infuse something with enough emotional energy that an item won't take a spell all that well."

I hadn't known that at all. Not that I spell a lot of my things. I tend to do more general spells rather than spells on certain items. I mean, some coffee shops might spell their cups, but for me it was easier to train folks to make good coffee than to spell a cup to make a person believe they were drinking good coffee. But I suppose what Julia was saying was essentially what I had always known, just not in those terms.

"So did the scarf need to be made by the person?" Natalie asked. "If so, who has a scarf just hanging around ready for a negative magic spell?"

"They wouldn't absolutely have to have made the scarf, but it's easier if they did. It's why witch crafters who use yarn can be so picky."

I remembered what I had heard about Chief Spader's wife. She made particularly fine yarn, very pure, from her goats. She made a lot selling it to other witches. If everyone who touched something added to the energy, then it would make sense that the more you did yourself, the easier the spells.

"It doesn't seem like machines would add energy," I said, thinking about it as I sipped my sweet tea.

"But people handle things before and after. And most of them are tired or unhappy because they don't want to be doing what they're doing," Julia said. "That adds energy. Trust me. I've spelled a lot of cloth."

I knew she had. I knew that before she quilted she washed the fabric and also did a spell to cleanse it. That made things easier for her. Got rid of conflicting energies to an extent, though nothing was perfect. And then she'd make the quilt and spell it if she was going to. I recalled that my mom would do the same type of spell as she wound yarn into balls from skeins.

"So someone at least had to have washed or treated the scarf before spelling it, which almost suggests they thought this murder through even before the fair," I said.

"Or they were wearing the scarf and they put the spell on when it happened. Having something for a long time can also add a layer of the person's energies making it easier to spell," Ashley said. She made it sound as if I were foolish for not knowing. I didn't work with craft items, so I didn't feel particularly foolish. I bet there were plenty of spells around familiars that she didn't know either.

"But it suggests at least some level of planning," Natalie said frowning. "I mean, yeah it could have been a crime of opportunity for a scarf-wearing person, but it's a nice day out today. I know some folks love scarves, but this was knit, so I don't think it was just a fashion statement."

"And it would have stood out if it was," I said, remembering the purples and blues of the scarf. The thick and wide scarf was the last item I'd have expected to be a murder weapon. It was more like the kind of thing Julia made for herself and her friends. In fact, when I thought about it, she had a scarf quite similar.

Julia glanced back and sighed. I turned and noted that Chief Spader was walking towards us.

"Julia Owlens, I need to take your statement about where you were this morning," Spader said formally.

My sister's face reddened. Ashley frowned.

People were turning around and looking. Normally our chief isn't so obvious about talking to someone, but it almost seemed like he wanted everyone to know he was talking to my sister. I wondered what that was about. Julia couldn't have had anything to do with this.

6

J ulia went off with Chief Spader. Ashley gave us a
look and then followed, though she maintained a
distance from them as if worried someone would
think she was walking with them. She was clearly
more worried about what people thought of her than she was
about Julia.

"Let's go over to the competition building," Natalie said,
standing up. She picked up her Diet Coke.

"I wonder why Chief Spader wants to talk to Julia?" I said.

"Call her tonight," Natalie advised. "She'll be done. And
maybe then she'll have talked to Tom, too, and she'll have
more information."

"She wasn't here this morning," I said. "She said that."

"Actually, she didn't," Natalie reminded me. "We sort of
assumed."

"Julia couldn't have done this!" I stopped where I was. A
few people looked at me, rather like I was a child having a
tantrum. Given my stance and Natalie's reaction, perhaps
I was.

"I never said that, either," Nat replied easily. She pulled me along.

"You know, it's possible they've asked Julia because she knows about crafts and they need clues. Chances are, she has insight into people who could at least knit the scarf even if she doesn't know if they do negative magic." Natalie kept her voice down and my arm tucked next to her so I couldn't pull away.

"But the way he did it…" It wasn't the usual casual, 'can I have a word' type thing. He'd spoken loudly and made people look at them.

"He might have wanted to let people know the police are on it. It's not as if he accused Julia or anything," Natalie said. "And really, we don't know where she was earlier."

I didn't like the implications. Chief Spader knew as well as anyone that people gossiped and such talk could cause problems for Julia at her work. She was up for a promotion in the fabric store she worked at and they'd be giving her more space to sell her quilts if she won the competition. A lot of that hinged on how she did at the fair. If, instead of winning a ribbon she had to talk to the chief of police, that could ruin her chances.

The competition building was gray brick and I hated the outside of it. It looked like someone had done their best to cross a prison building with a high school gymnasium and took the worst of both types of architecture. Inside, the place was better. The entry was wide and funneled people to either side to find seats in the stands. Restrooms were spaced along the side walls.

Those who were on the competition floor entered through doors in the back. There, they'd funnel through a maze of offices until they got to the doors to the competition floor. Just outside the building was a covered open area where the competitions for large animal familiars were held.

Natalie and I went to the right and through that door. In front of us were concrete stairs. The seats were wood benches, though in the middle area I noted blue chairs that looked like they would be at home in a nice baseball stadium.

We walked in front of mostly empty bleacher seats. A few people sat further up, almost to the ceiling, looking down. One was eating popcorn which I was no longer craving, having had an actual lunch.

There were more people in the blue seats, though even the middle area wasn't very packed. The far side was equally empty.

Below us, on the main floor, sat a bunch of wire kennels on tables that faced the doors we had entered through. Two cats were in those cages looking rather peeved, though I wasn't close enough to get an actual read on them. A couple of women stood around, one in a skirt and one in a nice pantsuit of the sort that was popular when my mom was a kid. My grandmother had worn them frequently in family pictures.

I noted the two women talking together. They seemed to know each other and there were plenty of smiles. I hoped that when the working feline class got in and they were waiting on others that people would talk and smile with each other there, too. Having had a murder, potentially because the woman was favored to win, made me concerned that there would be tension.

Natalie led me to a seat slightly behind a group of six women. They sat three in a lower row and three in a row right in front of us but they were clearly all together and were leaning over and talking. I had no doubt that's why Natalie chose our seats.

"I heard one judge for working felines is new," one of the younger women said. She might be my age or younger, her brown hair streaked with green and perfectly straight. She wore a windbreaker over a peach boat-neck sweater that went well with her particular skin tone.

Natalie pointedly didn't look at me. I angled myself so that they were less likely to notice the lanyard I wore.

"She's supposed to be very good," another woman said. "LaDona was singing her praises. Of course, with this incident, time will tell won't it? I mean, what if she decides to place a murderer?!"

"Not her fault," the oldest of the women said. Her hair was equally brown with a pink stripe down the back, almost skunk-like in its placement, but the lines on her face and the way her neck sort of waddled and moved suggested she was older than the others. "Judges are to judge the witches and their familiars, not determine who murdered someone. Even so, it might not be anyone from the class anyway."

"I doubt it," the woman who had said LaDona sang my praises jumped in. She wore her dark hair clipped short. It was so black I suspected she colored it. She wasn't terribly young either, though her face was firmer than the other woman. "I mean who else would want to murder Luanne?"

"Like she didn't piss off a bunch of witches," another woman said. I couldn't get a good look at her. She was short and sat at an angle.

The group muttered and talked about Luanne a bit. It seemed like no one particularly liked her.

"And Olivia was not looking forward to the overall working class competition. There are a couple of outstanding dog familiars to beat but Luanne and her cat were still favored," a silver-haired younger-looking woman said. Her skin was very fair and her eyes were light. The silver color looked good on her.

"Olivia and her horse can do anything those dogs can do and I can't imagine even Luanne and her cat would have done better." That was the older woman again. She gave a strict nod, then.

The woman who wanted to blame me if I placed a murderer started to say something.

The older woman broke in again, "Don't go pointing fingers at Olivia. I have no doubt she was over in the barn. And even if she wasn't, she's not the type to go around using negative magic."

Nods all around, except for the one woman who seemed to want drama.

Natalie and I remained quiet. Unfortunately, other entrants had come in and they were beginning to line up. I noticed one of the judging assistants out there which meant the competition was about to start.

While I knew Natalie was hoping to leave to discuss what we'd heard and probably look into this Olivia, I needed to stay. I was going to be a judge. I wanted to know how these three judges worked together. I'd be meeting the other working class judges tomorrow and we'd talk in a back room, our familiars present. I didn't want to be the one to drag out the process because I didn't understand. I hoped that by watching these judges with the casual feline class that I'd learn some pointers.

My heart started to pound thinking about being out on the floor in just a couple of days. While judging was an honor, I hoped it was one I could live up to.

7

I watched the three judges conferring. I noticed the way they all worked. First one judge, a skinny, older woman, gave directions and indicated which of the familiars should be brought to the examination table while another judge, this one a middle-aged woman who looked like a runner or mountain climber, went over the body shape and size. I knew they felt the body for general wellness and health and the fur to make sure the familiars were in good health.

I noticed that all three of the judge's familiars were sitting under the table. They would no doubt discuss lifestyle with each of the cats on the table. Familiars have a hard time lying to another one of their kind, so if a witch worked a cat too hard—not likely in this class—the familiar would say something.

The third judge, yet another woman, though this one older, with broad shoulders and close-cropped gray hair, hung back and let the other two work.

Once each of the fourteen familiars had been examined and were back in the kennels, the witches had to step back and the next part of the competition would begin. In the working class, the competition would be about working together. In this class, it was about having fun.

Each witch got a selection of cat toys to pick from. Once those were chosen the athletic-looking judge called time.

Each witch went to the kennel where their familiar waited and started swinging the toy. The other two judges went behind and made notes about which cats seemed to be having the most fun. The judges' familiars were all down under the table. They seemed more interested in the toys than in communicating with the other cats. They probably were, because cats, whether familiar or ordinary, are still cats.

After a minute, the judge who had said time called out stop. The witches all moved away from their familiars, and carefully toys in the waiting box before returning to their table a few feet from the kennels. The space between the table and the kennels was more important for working familiars but the leisure class also used the space.

The broad-shouldered judge then indicated to a single witch to go get her familiar. She brought her petite tuxedo cat back to the table.

The first judge announced that this would be a fun activity the two did together. Obviously, each witch had to make up a fun activity for herself and her cat. This witch did a patty-cake sort of game where she raised a hand and the cat touched it with a paw. The game got faster until the cat started using its nose. Finally, the witch used her nose as well and the two ended up giving each other nose kisses.

All three judges made notes. Each of them bent down to one of the feline familiars under the judging table. Clearly, the familiars had once again checked in with the competing feline.

Then the next witch got to go. I found the casual activities interesting. In working familiars, most activities were set and designed to determine the communication skills between witch and familiar. It was also designed to test how well the familiar and witch could work together.

Casual was about relaxing and playing. I wondered if these witches practiced the way the working classes practiced or if this class was less competitive.

Natalie fidgeted next to me. The women in front of us were mostly quiet. Even when they had a comment, one of them would whisper to another.

I got up and started to leave, Natalie close behind.

I didn't say a word until we were out. I know that audiences whisper but it's always nice to have quiet when you're the one doing the competing. Most witches and their familiars need to be touching to connect telepathically but for those that don't need to touch, having a quiet area makes it easier to connect simply because it's easier to concentrate.

"We ought to find Olivia," Natalie said the moment we were out the main doors.

"Horse barn?" I asked. Natalie nodded. We headed across the way to the barns. The one closest to the parking lot had horses. The other two had various other large animals, including goats and sheep and even a handful of cows, though cows weren't popular as familiars.

We were nearly to the barn when Flori came out with her aunt.

"Jade!" Flori said. Her face practically glowed. "I think I talked to one of the barn cats!"

"Like a familiar?" I asked.

Nadine, Flori's witch "cousin" shook her head. "Just some telepathy. The barn cat is an ordinary." Her eyes were sort of hooded at that, but I understood her concern.

Flori had gotten magic from another witch using a forbidden spell to steal the magic from one witch and giving it to her. The original spell was for a familiar, but even that was considered negative magic. Taking magic from a familiar meant taking a life. It was ironic that Flori could apparently connect with an ordinary feline. Or course, having been ordinary herself and just enhanced, so to speak, perhaps that would be a unique talent that she had.

"He said he liked the way I rubbed his ears!" Flori was practically jumping up and down. "I didn't think I'd be able to hear a familiar or if one would choose me, but now I know what to look for!"

Familiars were the ones who chose their witch and they did so when they let them connect telepathically. Running the cat café, I knew to look for such signs, though not all familiars immediately warmed up to someone. Still, if a witch really loved a feline, we usually did paperwork and asked them back if the cat hadn't initiated contact. Mason would talk to the familiar about the witch wanting to adopt them. I never sent cats out to homes they weren't interested in going to.

Flori, as she was when she first came into the café, wasn't someone I even wanted in the building. In fact, I'd kicked her out. But this new Flori, the one who now understood what was happening to her, was a completely different person and I suspected that one of our cats would bond with her, though I hoped she liked one of our mature and outgoing familiars. She had too much energy for a quieter cat like Jelliane.

"I heard about the death," Nadine said. "Do you know any more?"

I shook my head. I probably knew more than she did, but I wasn't sure what was fact and what was gossip.

"I wondered seeing I heard she was supposed to be in your competition category. Most people wouldn't care, but LaDona can be a bear about the way things look and she's having a fit about how it would look if you happened to place murderer."

"She talked to me," I said. "I felt like she expected me to solve the murder myself or something."

Nadine nodded. "I'm sorry. It's such an honor to be picked to be a judge, but what a stressful thing to have happen. It's not like you're the only judge out there. I'm sure the others got their own orders, but it probably feels worse because this is your first time."

"Thanks," I said. She was right. It did feel like my entire judge career was on the line. I hadn't even known I wanted to be a judge until it seemed it might be taken away as quickly as it had been given.

"You'll figure it out," Flori said. "Lina even said you were a huge help in figuring out what happened to me. You'll be great!"

It was nice to know someone had confidence in me.

8

The horse barn had the overwhelming musky smell of horses, not to mention the pungent stink of manure. It felt warmer inside than I expected. The barns were far more open than the vendor and craft buildings, but despite the openness, they held heat more effectively, probably due to all the large animals. The horses had two aisles with small stalls on either side of each aisle.

Instead of sawdust, hay covered the ground with even more of it in the stalls. Each horse had its own stall. The walls to either side of them went up nearly to the ceiling and were solid. The front had a gate that came up to about my waist. Once, the wood had been painted white. Now it was a dirty cream.

I heard plenty of people talking. About half the horses had an owner with them. The ones that didn't were being looked after by a human neighbor. I had no doubt the witches had worked out with each other who would watch the familiars while they ran to the little girl's room or ran and got more food.

Ordinary folks loved the large animals, the horses in

particular. I knew that plenty of our local horse farms relied on people at the fair coming to check out their breed lines and asking about stud fees and such. Not all the inquiries were from witches and inquiries from ordinaries were always given just as much consideration.

As a cat person, I knew familiar to familiar breeding typically resulted in a familiar with good magical talents. Having worked in shelters, I understood that canines were different. The best canine familiars came from either one canine familiar and one ordinary or two ordinary canines with magic in their ancestry. I wasn't sure about horses.

Given how lucrative horse breeding was for our local farms, I had a feeling that a familiar didn't necessarily sire a familiar when paired with an ordinary horse.

Naturally, there were always exceptions and familiars turned up in the oddest places, often spontaneously. For instance, there were stories of hunters being contacted by deer who had magic. Now and then a gardener might be out in their yard and get chosen by a wild rabbit. Sometimes these pairings became witch and familiar, but in others, the two just had a moment and let the relationship go.

I was drawn to a dabble gray on the left side of the aisle. No one was with her. I read her stats and rubbed her nose. She snorted at me and nuzzled to see if I had any treats. I was sorry I didn't.

Natalie glanced back and frowned at me. She was clearly reading the informational signs on each stall, hoping to find an owner named Olivia. I reluctantly moved away from the dapple.

Up ahead, a young man, barely out of his teens, and a woman not much older were talking in low voices. I tried to make out what they were saying but couldn't. When we got closer I heard her say, "You overfeed all the time, Ian!"

I smiled a little at myself. They were arguing about food

when I'd been certain the argument had been about the murder.

Natalie and I got to the end of the first aisle and didn't find Olivia's name associated with any of the horses. I paused and petted a lovely, sleek gray cat. I wondered if this was the tom that had talked to Flori.

I reached out with my magic, but Flori's aunt had been right if this was the cat. He was definitely ordinary. He liked the people around here and the warmth of the horses, which he knew he'd miss soon enough. He'd lived in the fair barn for several years catching mice and enjoying the company while it lasted.

He didn't speak to me so much as I got the sense of contentment around the thoughts. Images of things came to mind. It wasn't the sort of communication I had with Mason. I wondered if Flori got this sort of sense and thought they had "talked" or if he really had spoken with her the way I might speak to Mason.

After pausing for the cat, which Natalie also did, giving him an ear rub making his toes flex into what I call *making biscuits*, we continued around the corner to the next aisle. I noted the folding chairs outside the stalls though some people sat on the low wall between the horse and the aisle. A few sat inside. It had been the same on the other aisle but it seemed like there were more chairs here, placed further into the aisle. This aisle was a more social place than the other side.

A few owners stopped Natalie and me as we looked at the names on the doors. They asked if we had horse familiars, which we both acknowledged with a negative. Trinity had been the one in our group to be horse crazy. She still rode, though her familiar wasn't a horse. At the moment, Trinity didn't have a familiar. She'd had a guinea pig in college but it had died and she'd not re-bonded with another.

It took some witches time to get over the loss of a familiar. The bond is intense. In Trinity's case, I think that she'd moved past the grief and just wasn't sure of the type of familiar she wanted.

Trinity was passionate about horses, but I think she saw drawbacks to having one as a familiar. First and foremost, living in an apartment meant that she'd have to keep her familiar in a barn that wasn't hers. She liked dogs and cats as well, but I saw her with a larger dog. Even Tyson's boxer was a bit smaller than the canine I pictured Trinity with.

About halfway down on the right, I noted a stately black thoroughbred with his head out the opening. A woman with curly red hair was feeding him a piece of carrot. Something about the way she moved suggested they were practicing something. I knew even before Natalie and I got there that we'd found Olivia.

"Hi," I said, glancing at the name to see Olivia Coombs though I had had no doubt that this was the woman we were looking for.

"Hey," Olivia said. It didn't take her long to notice my lanyard.

"Working felines, huh?" she smiled. "I do working horses, but in competition not as a judge. I figure I want to get three firsts as overall working familiar and then I'll look into judging."

"I know cats," I said. "I work with my feline familiar or he works with me depending upon who you talk to."

Olivia had the grace to laugh at that.

"It's one thing about horses. They don't have to be in charge. Probably why I've got a horse familiar and not a cat. I like being equal, you know?"

I nodded. I got that. It was an interesting take on horses versus cats or even dogs, which tended to be more childlike in their bonding.

"Sorry to hear about Luanne," Olivia said. "I would have liked going up against her in the ring, just to prove that I could. I can't believe someone murdered her. I even heard it was negative magic."

"I was in the group that sort of found her," I said. I mean I hadn't really found her. I'd just been part of the group looking at her. "It was pretty horrible."

Natalie had stayed quiet to this point. "Most people appreciate having the competition gone," she said.

Olivia gave her an odd look. "I thrive on the competition I like knowing where my weaknesses are. Besides, different judges look at different things. I might just live up in Midway, but Bolivar is a good traveler and he's willing."

"Do you work together at your day job?" I asked.

"I work at the school for my day job, but I also give riding lessons. Bolivar helps me when he senses the student is about to do something another horse wouldn't tolerate, not that he's all that tolerant, but at least I know what he's reacting to. I mostly know anyway, but it's nice to get it from the horse's mouth, so to speak." Olivia laughed at her pun which was clearly intentional.

"You must work really well together. So many of the working familiars work full-time with their witch," I said. I sincerely did admire her for that.

Olivia shrugged. "At some point, I'd love to create a healing program with Bolivar. I've watched programs where horses work with people helping them with various psychological issues. I've had some aches and pains and Bolivar seems to help me. He says he's not doing anything, but I feel it in my body. I'd love to get together with a natural healer and see if that talent is repeatable."

"You have time," Natalie said, eyeing Bolivar. He wasn't all that old in horse years, his coat still shiny and his stance sturdy and eager.

Olivia nodded. "He's easy-going for his age and breed. Most thoroughbreds are temperamental and I'm not going to say that Bol doesn't like things his way, he's just a little less persnickety about it."

"As I'm not judging your class, I can wish you luck," I said with a smile.

Olivia laughed and Natalie and I left.

"So you do think she's really that okay with competition or was that deflecting?" Natalie asked as we got towards the far end of the barn.

"She seemed genuine," I said, wondering. I tried to imagine Olivia working with negative magic but I just couldn't quite do it.

"You're too trusting," Natalie said firmly. "You need to look at motives and figure out why someone would tell you things like that."

Quite honestly I had no desire to act as if someone was out to get me. Even if staying a judge did depend upon me figuring out how not to place someone who might have murdered one of the people in my competition.

I sighed as I walked out of the barn. My phone rang just then. I answered and it was Tom Alsez. He wanted to speak to me in the competition building.

9

Natalie insisted on going with me, although I knew Tom wanted to chat with me alone. He was working out of one of the offices towards the back of the competition building. I had to lead Natalie around to the far side, between the covered outdoor ring and the concrete walls. In the back facing the parking lot, we followed a sawdust-lined path riddled with weeds until we came to an exterior door. Inside, a long hallway faced us, lined with doors.

I heard only the low murmur of conversation behind one of the doors. I wondered if we were between competitions when workers cleaned out kennels and made sure everything was as sterile as possible for the next set of familiars or if the building was just that quiet in the back.

I kept walking until I found Tom working out of a large conference room. Some businesses rented space at the fairgrounds for meetings, and I wondered if this was that room. The table inside was as big as my apartment. In fact, it was probably as long as my entire café, with upholstered chairs on casters all around it. Tom sat at the end nearest the door.

"Thanks for coming so quickly," Tom said standing up. He wasn't terribly handsome but he felt grounded, his body stocky and solid. His short brown hair had evidently been recently trimmed because I noticed parts of his scalp shining through the cut.

The black uniform of the department hugged his muscular arms tightly enough that I wondered how hard it would be for him to draw his gun if he had to.

"I didn't think I should just wander around if you were waiting," I said.

"You'd be amazed at the people who do," Tom said. "I've got most of the observers identified from the images. I don't suppose you and Natalie knew anyone else who was there?"

I shook my head. I hadn't noticed anyone I knew.

"I think I saw Lyn Upton in the crowd," Natalie said.

I was surprised. I hadn't noticed Lyn.

Tom made a note. "I had her already, but thanks."

So much for my powers of observation. Of course, I'd been focused on the body and not on the people in the crowd. Perhaps Natalie managed to look around and check out the people around us.

"I'm going to talk to Jade first, if you don't mind?" Tom asked, looking at Natalie.

Natalie sort of huffed, but she left the conference room without much of an argument.

"We ran into Lina, one of the WBI witches, just as we were leaving the craft building," I said. "I gave her a statement right then."

Tom gave a thin smile. "While they'll get your statement from me, too, I doubt I'll get to see theirs."

I nodded. It was too bad the WBI was so cagey about their information. I could have understood it if everyone on our police force was ordinary, but Waverton had so many witches and familiars that the department only hired witches. I guess at various times they had tried an ordinary rookie and attempted to keep them out of witch business, but it never worked out.

Tom asked what I knew. I talked about being over at the craft building and running into Luanne, who I didn't know at the time. I talked about how she seemed very critical of the quilt we were in front of. I described it again and said it wasn't Julia's, just in case he might think I had taken offense to Luanne's comments.

I said I had felt weird so I started to leave and ran into Natalie. We were perusing the quilts when we heard a scream and went back to see what had happened. I left out a lot of the things that Lina had pulled out of me when I talked to her, but I figured that would just please Tyson when I talked to him.

I wasn't volunteering anything, like say, why I was in the craft building.

Tom didn't ask me about what I was doing in that particular building, probably assuming I had just been enjoying the fair for the morning. If he did see Lina's report or found out what had happened with Lyn some other way, I could just say I didn't think of it. It's not like he asked. Lyn might be a suspect, but I wasn't going to try pointing fingers at her again, though now that I thought of it, it was odd that she was there.

He did clarify a few things, like what I had noticed around the body, the fact that I was well aware that there was negative magic around.

"I'm not sure what judges know about entrants and I'm wondering if you heard anything about Luanne," he said.

"Not before that. I got some general information on the entrants but I didn't spend time with it in case knowing more about them influenced how I saw them. I'd have thought that would be true for all the judges. It's easier to be less biased if you don't know people," I said. Not that that was working out. About the only person who hadn't tried to sway me was Olivia. Of course, I wasn't judging her class so maybe it wasn't worth her time.

Seeing Olivia with her horse, reminded me of the horse quilt. I was going to have to go back and see who made it. After all, that was the one Luanne had been criticizing. It seemed pertinent that it was a horse quilt and enhanced the bond with the familiar through magic.

Tom wrote down what I'd told him while my brain was taking me down these lanes of inquiry. I couldn't wait to talk more to Natalie.

"What do you know now?" he asked, giving me a look that was almost as intense as that of a WBI witch.

I couldn't not tell him what I'd learned about Luanne's questionable practices in her job, the fact that she was critical about a lot of things, and that she was favored to win the feline working class competition, which I was judging.

Tom took his time writing all that down, though I knew he magically recorded everything. Finally, when he finished, he asked if I knew anything else. I decided that while I had lots of questions and theories, I didn't actually know anything else, so I said no.

With that, I was free to leave so he could talk to Natalie. We changed places and I got to pace in the hallway. I wondered what Nat had done. I didn't notice any wear on the floor and the way Natalie paces when she's waiting you'd think that would happen.

I tended to walk more slowly, first in one direction down the hallway and then the other. I passed the cream walls and my footsteps squeaked every third step on the vinyl flooring. I passed doors to offices, some of which were open. Several rooms had desks around the edges. Three, as if they were already prepared for judges.

Tomorrow, I'd be in one of those rooms with the two other judges I had yet to meet. I hoped by then there would be leads in the murder. I wondered if LaDona had warned the other judges about placing a murderer or if she had only spoken to me because I was the new judge. Like I had to have more instruction than anyone else because I was the most junior person there. You'd think that would allow me some leeway, but alas it seemed it did not.

Finally, Natalie came out of the conference room and found me. We hurried outside to the fairgrounds.

"I told him what we heard about Olivia," Natalie said. "Why didn't you?"

"He didn't ask. He asked what I knew and I didn't know anything about her. I just heard things," I said.

"Well now he's wondering if you're lying to him for some reason," Natalie said. "And he's not pleased."

"Look, he didn't ask specifically what I had heard or thought. He asked what I knew. Tyson has told me that I shouldn't just blurt everything I know out to the police, even the police I know, like Tom. It's best to let them ask specific questions and offer information then," I said.

"I'm sure that's good advice if you're a suspect," Natalie began.

"Tyson says that you never know when you go from being a witness to a person of interest to a suspect." I leaped in and cut her off. Natalie likes to think she knows stuff, but sometimes she steps out of what she really knows.

Instead of an argument, I got a shrug, which meant she was deferring to Tyson's education and background even if she wasn't exactly thrilled to do it.

The sky was starting to pink, which meant it was getting late in the afternoon. I glanced at my phone and then at Natalie.

"It looks like I need to get back. I wanted to put the café

familiars to bed and then I need to spend some time with Mason. He's not used to being apart from me all day like this," I said.

"And I'll do some more sleuthing at the hotel. I'll see who's staying there and what I can find out. Luanne was there, I'm sure, so I'll know where she's from and maybe that will help with some background." Natalie hurried me towards the parking area.

I had to break off to go to the smaller parking lot where judges got to park. There were some good perks about being a judge. Now, if only LaDona decided I was worthy of keeping them.

Charlene, one of my regular café workers, had already gotten most of the familiars settled in their evening kennels. Mason was still out in the feline room of the café. I loved that area. While the front was all dark wood that I'd left from the former tavern, along with deep red fabric accents—that, of course, had black and white tuxedo cats—the feline room was more lightly done, more upbeat.

I always felt soothed back there, even when the music was already off. Charlene and Greg were finishing cleaning the front. We were open for a few more minutes but I doubted anyone else would come by. That's one nice thing about running a coffee shop. You might have to start early, but you also got out equally early in the evening.

Noting that all the current familiars were settled, I looked at them, wondering if any of them would be good with Flori. Alcari, a small male Siamese was testy. He and Flori were a little too much alike and I had a feeling that magic would fly, and not in a good way, if the two of them were together.

The older calico, Jelliane, was too retiring for Flori, or I thought so. She didn't like conflict. If she could have handled that, I probably would have adopted her out months ago, but she could get in timid moods. Oddly, there were days when she didn't seem shy at all, but others when she barely stuck her head out of her kennel and only joined the other cats in the café when Mason agreed to guard her.

Ned was tiny but he might be a good fit, though I wasn't at all certain. The newest familiar was a large gray shorthair named Twillingham. His big rounded face and equally round golden eyes suggested British shorthair rather than American. He acted British as well, so I was certain that was why his original witch had given him that name.

Unfortunately, like so many of these familiars, the original witch had died and Twillingham had made his way from Boston to me, here in Waverton. I felt badly for him because ordinary friends had been trying to adopt him out until he made a call for help that another witch's familiar had heard and he'd been brought to me.

Twillingham was very territorial and he and Mason had a few clashes, which had never happened before. Mason wasn't at all fond of Twillingham and the feeling, according to Mason, was mutual. However, they did their best to settle themselves in different parts of the café. Because of that, I really wanted him to get adopted, but again, I wasn't sure if Flori was the right person.

Over the last week, I'd noticed that Twillingham seemed more interested in my male guests than in the females, so that would probably leave Flori out, although cats will always surprise you.

As Charlene called out a good-bye, I waved and settled into my favorite brown microfiber café chair. It blended well with the pale greens and made a perfect accent, bringing in the darker browns from the front to the back. Mason immediately leaped on my lap for some snuggles and to catch up before I went back to the office to check on the receipts.

Charlene would have told me if there were any problems.

How was the fair? Mason thought at me.

We were telepathically bonded but I had to be touching him to hear him, at least with any clarity. There were spells I could do to let me hear him from further away, but I've always figured why waste magic when it was just as easy to run my fingers through Mason's plush ginger and white fur.

"A woman, one of the women entered in the feline working class, was murdered there this morning. I saw her," I said. I often spoke out loud to Mason, unless I had people in the café who would overhear the conversation.

Did you see who did it? Mason asked. He stretched out across my lap, his head dropping lower between my thigh and the arm of the chair. I didn't see how that could possibly be comfortable.

"I didn't. I do have some thoughts. I would have anyway, but LaDona put pressure on me to make sure I didn't let a murderer win the competition," I said.

Who do you think did it? Mason asked. *You did a good job finding out who really killed Trinity's boss.*

I wasn't sure I agreed with Mason's assessment. I sort of stumbled into something when I found that killer.

"There were dog people who thought the woman was favored to win. Someone else suggested a horse person named Olivia, but she seems really nice so I doubt it's her. And then there are the cat people. I mean even Lyn Upton from high school was talking to me about her familiar and how she looked forward to seeing me in the competition. Like she was buttering me up."

In your books, it's always the person you least suspect, so you should probably tell the police about Olivia, Mason advised.

"Natalie already did. Tom Alsez took information from

me this afternoon. I didn't mention her because Tyson has told me to not tell the police anything that they don't specifically ask about and Tom didn't specifically ask," I said. "But it reminds me, I want to know who made the quilt Luanne was criticizing when I talked to her."

You talked to the dead woman? Mason demanded like I had left that part out.

I had to explain to him more about my morning and talking to people. I looked up the fair's website to see quilt entries. I found the name of the person who had made the horse quilt. Shannon Coombs made it.

"It looks the same last name as Olivia made the quilt that Luanne was criticizing. They're probably related, but I can't imagine that someone would kill over criticism about a quilt, particularly when I doubt it will place. It's nice, but Julia's is better and there's another one that might even be better than hers, though I don't like it quite as well," I said. I mean, I owed my sister some loyalty, and her particular subject, which included inspiration from Mason, was near and dear to my heart.

Then, there you have it. It's probably Olivia or her relative. I mean, it sounds like this person was a problem for both of them. Mason leaned up and began washing his side, just missing the half of a ginger-colored heart that lay on that side of his body.

"I have no proof," I said.

Just don't place them. Mason moved from the white area by the heart to his belly, bringing a paw up onto his side while he washed that area.

I rolled my eyes, certain my familiar wasn't watching me. I wouldn't place them because I didn't place canines or equines. I only placed felines. Without proof, I couldn't be certain that the murderer wasn't a witch with a feline familiar.

I'm still listening, Mason assured me. He didn't miss a beat on his bath and put his paw down only when he was ready. Then I got the glare of annoyance because my world wasn't quite as simple as his.

"Look, I have to be certain I don't place a feline familiar and a witch who might have murdered this woman. And it seems like this is pretty competitive as far as the witches entering. I had no idea," I said. "I thought, sometimes, that we should enter, but figured I didn't know what I was doing and didn't want to embarrass us. Now, having seen how people react, I'm glad I didn't. I can't imagine taking the contest that seriously. I mean, as a judge, I'll take things seriously and look closely at all the cats and their witches and how they work together, but actually entering seems out of my league."

Not mine. Mason turned himself over to get the other side of his belly.

"Too bad you're stuck with me," I told him.

Mason didn't bother to answer.

I pulled up information on my phone that LaDona had sent me. I had purposely not looked too closely at the entrants. I didn't want to prejudge anyone or be accused of it but with the murder hanging over my head, I needed to find out more.

I learned that with Luanne there were fifteen entrants in the working feline class. That was more than I expected. I didn't have numbers of canines or any of the other familiars but I expected there were even more dogs. Thankfully, I wouldn't be judging them.

I bit my lip as I read names. Lyn's name stood out and a couple of others. I recognized the name Desiree Morning. She didn't live in Waverton but our families were friends and she'd stayed at our house when I was a little girl. She babysat Julia and me when we were little and the adults went out to dinner and a show or, more likely, to a bar to socialize.

I hadn't seen Desiree in years. I would have loved to have caught up, but I probably couldn't say much until after the competition was over.

The other names were just names from around town and people I knew slightly from having worked at the Waverton shelter before opening the café. Mark Wells was a Maine Coon breeder, I knew, and Joe Fitzgerald worked at the local college. There were likely other people I would know when I saw them.

I couldn't imagine any of them murdering someone, yet I would have said Lyn wasn't the sort to stop me in the middle of the fair and try to ingratiate herself, either. Not that there was really any parallel to making nice with a judge and killing the competition. It was just that it made me realize that people would do things I didn't expect them to do.

My phone rang and I picked it up. Mason began to purr, signaling he was aware that my caller was Tyson. I settled in for a nice chat with my boyfriend, something that still sent a thrill down my spine, even if boyfriend sounded a bit too high school for our relationship.

The next morning when I got to the fair, I had Mason with me. I had a meeting with the other judges at nine. Mason was in his carrier and I carried a bunch of items that I wanted him to have with him in the sterile kennel that sat in the judges' offices. I worried a bit about the cats at the café without Mason there, but most of them had been there long enough that they knew the ropes.

Getting to the competition building was slower with a big cat carrier and all the items I had packed up. I wasn't the only one with a lot of stuff. I noticed one of the canine judges walking in with two bags and a leash wrapped around her wrist, a small white dog trotting beside her. While familiars weren't likely to run off, I knew that the fair had rules about familiars not under obvious control. I suspected it had something to do with liability insurance that wasn't specific to witches, seeing we did have ordinary people coming through.

The morning smelled of cinnamon, probably from the booth in the food dome that made cinnamon rolls. My mouth watered thinking about them. I'd had some coffee from down at the café and a muffin before I'd come in, but fair food always makes my stomach perk up and go hmm.

The low murmur of conversation enveloped me as I got onto the grounds. The slight hum of the machines that ran the rides greeted me as the carnies in the midway tested their wares. I heard someone yell from back there.

The day was barely starting, though I felt a sense of anticipation on the part of everyone. Today, the craft judges would be officially tallying their scores. My group would be on deck in the morning, working out who would do what during the judging and perhaps having a mock run-through. Our familiars would all get to know one another.

In the afternoon we'd have another meeting and Saturday we'd be up judging the feline working class. Saturday was a prime day, but the event wasn't at a prime time. The canines were late afternoon when people were winding down from exploring the fair. We were at noon. Most people who were at the fair would probably come in and take a look. Probably more now that someone had been murdered and everyone seemed to know all about it.

I sighed heavily as I slipped inside the backdoor. A bald sexless person stood at the door in a dark outfit that could have been a tunic over pants or skirt, I couldn't quite tell. They nodded at me seeing my lanyard.

I smiled, or hoped I smiled and didn't grimace, at them as I went in. Mason moved in his carrier putting me slightly off-balance.

Cool air from inside the building hit me, raising a few goosebumps. The slight sense of humidity outside, probably because we were going to get rain, dissipated.

I set down one of my bags of items and pulled my phone from my pocket and checked my assignment. Judging room 14-B. I headed down the hallway looking at room numbers.

My shoes squeaked against the floor. I heard voices coming from a couple of closed doors. While the hall was empty, it seemed busier in the building than it had yesterday. I passed the conference room entrance, which was closed up. I noticed a sign that said police only. I was tempted to see if the door was locked but my hands were full and if someone were inside, I had no idea what I'd say.

Finally, I found room 14-B, which was next to another door labeled 14-A. Both doors were open. A appeared to be the size of a closet, but fortunately, the room I was in was sized like the rooms I'd seen yesterday. I walked in, startled when I noticed someone else in the room, at the desk facing the wall that held the door.

I didn't recognize the man, even from the café, which suggested he was from out of town. His blue-black hair was combed back and looked like it was naturally straight. It fell to the bottom of his ears. He had cheekbones so prominent they could have cut glass. His nose was narrow and long. Eyes that were so dark they looked almost black stared at me, equally startled, from a face with skin several shades darker than mine.

I noted the white button-down shirt and bolero tie that hung at a slightly awkward angle. The cowboy boots below nicely pressed jeans completed the look.

"I'm Jade Owlens, one of the judges," I said. A cat meowed from the kennel nearest that desk. It was the largest cat I'd ever seen, outside of the Maine Coons. This one was a black and gray tabby, with stripes so even it had to have been bred by a quality breeder. It glowed with health.

"Ben Smith," he said holding his hand out and then dropping it as he noticed all my things.

"It's nice to meet you," I said. I moved towards the back and took the desk next to his. I put down Mason, which made me feel much more able to move.

"This is Mason," I said pointing to the carrier. "My familiar."

"This is Night Shadow." He pointed at the large cat in the kennel. Night Shadow looked up at me, meeting my eyes with his, no, *her* very green ones. I could get lost in those eyes. For a moment, I almost envied Ben.

"She's gorgeous." For some reason, although I had initially thought the cat was male, I knew she was female.

"Most people think she's a male," Ben said, approving. Perhaps Night Shadow had let me know she was female.

I put one of the blankets in the kennel. They had small litter boxes and I made sure that was on the far side. I pulled out the water dish so that I wouldn't forget to fill it. Then I put in a nice bed that Mason likes to curl up in.

"I haven't done this before," I said.

"Judy Pearl was supposed to judge, but she was unexpectedly taken ill," Ben said, almost formally. He wasn't that much older than I was. "I heard they had gotten someone local. Not everyone wants to travel to the Midwest any longer so there is definitely a need for more judges here. I don't fly with Night Shadow nowadays. Too much hassle, but she doesn't mind a car ride. Not all cats are as easy going."

I couldn't imagine a cat who looked less easy-going than his Night Shadow. Clearly, she was a master of deception. I wondered how that fit with how Ben saw himself.

I got Mason's kennel as set up as I could and then I let him out to put him in the kennel.

"He's a very fine cat," Ben said. "And you work with him?"

"I run the familiar café in town," I said.

"Ah! Jade's. Like your name. I had thought it was a tribute to the stone." Ben looked down and away as if embarrassed he'd said that.

"I suppose it might have been in a roundabout way," I

said. "My parents did name me Jade because it was my grandmother's favorite stone."

Ben pursed his lips and looked thoughtful. I wondered if he were one of those people who got impressions from small tidbits of information. Some witches did. I didn't, at least not consciously, though every now and again I'd just know something about someone.

Mason turned around and sniffed at everything in the kennel, making sure it was to his satisfaction.

I asked Ben where I could find water and took the water dish out to the hallway and turned right. Apparently, there was a small kitchen a few doors down and they had filtered water. I noticed another man walking with a large tote but not a familiar. I wondered if he weren't a judge or if had already left his familiar in the judging room.

I started to greet him, but he passed by without so much as a wave. I could have been a wall for all that he noticed me. Actually, he'd have noticed a wall standing in his way more than he paid attention to me.

I returned to Mason, Ben, and Night Shadow. After I put the water dish in the kennel I sat in the chair and looked around.

"Do you and Night Shadow work together?" I asked.

"Not quite like you and Mason," Ben said. "I'm a writer. Night Shadow has input into my stories. I write speculative fiction."

"Wow!" I didn't know what else to say. The idea of meeting a writer was sort of intimidating. I read, sure, but I'd never actually tried to write and the idea of making up an entire story felt like it would be difficult. I mean, I always made up stories in my head usually without even realizing it, but to put something like that down on paper…that would be a whole different thing.

"It's not quite a wow," Ben said. "It's more like I sit at a computer and put words down when I'm not actively judging cat shows. I also do the write-ups for most of the competitions, at least for the felines. It's one reason I'm early. I wanted to get the basics of yesterday's competitions."

"Ours might be a little more interesting than usual what with one of the entrants being murdered," I said.

Ben nodded, seriously, looking sad. "Luanne has competed in this class before. I didn't know her exactly, but I've encountered her. A difficult woman. I feel for her familiar, though. They were close."

"More so than most familiars?" I asked. I didn't mean to belittle the loss, but in general, the bond between witch and familiar was very tight.

"Oh yeah," Ben said. "They worked together daily and then worked on competing. I'm sure you'd find it hard to have Mason talking to you all day and then spending hours working on your skills where he's telepathically speaking to you. Luanne didn't seem to have an issue."

I looked up at the ceiling thinking about what it would be like if Mason was always commenting on what I did or did not do. He certainly had his own opinions about everything and I didn't always agree, something that always surprised him, as if he couldn't conceive of me having my own thoughts and opinions.

Ben laughed at my reaction. "Yeah. I think every witch with a feline would get it. Cats do have opinions and they aren't shy about sharing them, particularly when our actions fall a bit short."

"But Luanne was okay with being that telepathically bonded to her cat?" I asked.

"Her witch-line had some psychic abilities and I guess she worked at it with animals. She did animal communication. Of course, her familiar reached out and helped her, so she was popular," Ben said.

"I heard that she did that," I said. "It seemed sort of questionable, at least the way I was trained."

"It was. And the WBI kept an eye on her. However, she coached her words such that ordinaries always thought she was just particularly good at communicating with their pets. And her familiar wasn't always able to connect with an ordinary animal, so there were times when she could give only the usual vague impressions. I know that some of the competition folks were uncomfortable when she entered because part of the contest is promoting the best of the best and they didn't agree with her ethical choices," Ben said.

"I can't say that LaDona gave me anything about ethics in judging." It would explain why she was so adamant that I didn't place a murderer and her fears about how that would look. It seemed like such considerations would have been part of the judging handbook I had gotten. I would have looked more closely at the familiars and their witches sooner had I known.

"Waverton is an unusual situation. It's a fair which entices ordinaries, though most ignore the competition building thanks to spells. However, it's considered a less prestigious competition to win because of the fair situation and the entry qualifications aren't as high. That's not to put it down or anything," Ben added quickly.

"Not offended," I said. "I've never been one for competitions. I mean, sometimes I'd go watch the ones here, particularly the felines because I've always been drawn to cats. I was surprised when LaDona asked me about judging."

Ben stepped over and glanced out the door and then looked back at me. "Rumor has it that you had an in with the WBI and LaDona was hoping to capitalize on that."

I opened my mouth not sure what to say. Fortunately, my body took over and I started laughing. When I was able to catch my breath, which was not an immediate thing, I shook my head in awe of the idiocy, if that was true about LaDona.

"Me? An in with the WBI? Only if they think I'm a suspect," I said. "I had to talk to them when some...er...thing broke into my café and I was nearly killed by a witch they were searching for. This time, I happened to be in the same building as Luanne when she was murdered and I was grilled by one of the WBI witches before I could even leave."

Ben chuckled with me. "See? Rumors."

"Rumors. Although I have no idea exactly why LaDona picked me."

"You run your own business working with your familiar. You know what you can expect from working with a feline. I think that's what got all of us started in judging, at least in this category. Casual and luxury classes are pretty much who you know." Ben shrugged like this was no big deal.

Just then a very fat woman came rushing in carrying her familiar in a carrier much like Mason's and a large bag with blankets falling out of it. Her hair was bleached white blonde and cut very short. Her round face was cheery, but she looked a bit harried.

"Sorry. Got the wrong parking lot and had to move the car," she said. Though she appeared to have been running, she wasn't the least bit out of breath.

"Hey Deena," Ben said. "You haven't been to Waverton before?"

"Not to judge," Deena said, setting the cat carrier down and taking a look around. "No group table, but individual computers. Interesting. I both like it and hate it."

Ben chuckled again, an easy and familiar laugh that said he and Deena had worked together before and understood each other's foibles.

"I'm Deena," the woman said reaching a hand out to me.

"Jade. I'm new." Although if Deena were like Ben, she probably knew that.

"So I heard. LaDona spoke very highly of you. You have a coffee shop in town and your familiar works there?" Deena bent down to settle her familiar into the kennel by the final desk.

"It's a café like cat cafes, only, this being Waverton, all my felines are familiars. Most of them have lost to witches to death, a couple to dementia, though most familiars stick around through that, and one just wasn't a good fit. Now and then a breeder will have trouble placing a familiar and I get it as well," I explained.

"What about ordinaries?" Deena asked.

"They come in and enjoy the cats. Sometimes I get inquiries. If the familiar is older, some of them will consider an ordinary person. Mason says they think of it like retirement."

"Mason? Your familiar?" Deena checked, looking up at me from where she'd settled on the floor putting in a blanket and some toys for her cat, which I noticed had long, flowing creamy gold and orange fur.

I nodded.

"Interesting. I like that you can service ordinaries without giving away that you're a witch. I know Waverton has so much hidden, but I like the hiding in plain sight. How do you tell someone the cat doesn't want them?"

"If they're ordinary, mostly I'll say I have another adopter. If they come back, I do have someone who can change a memory slightly so that they think that they forgot to ask and I can make up something else."

Deena nodded. "You heard about the murdered woman?" she asked, pushing herself up from her knees.

"We've been talking about it," Ben said. "What did you expect?"

Deena smiled. It came easily to her face, quickly reaching her eyes in fondness.

"I can't say I liked Luanne. I know she's good. I've given her decent marks in other competitions, but I kind of hated it. I'm sure she loved getting to me," Deena said. "Still, I wouldn't have wished her dead, just that she'd have a sudden aversion to competitions or something."

Ben nodded at that.

"Why didn't you like her?" I asked. "I sort of talked to her, without realizing who I was talking to in the craft building, but…"

Deena sighed. "It's horrible to speak ill of the dead. I should be better than that. But let's face it, Luanne was difficult. She sent me all sorts of missives about what I wasn't doing correctly in judging, even though I'd been judging longer than she'd been entering. She made faces while other entrants were having one-on-ones with the feline judge. She'd been known to sit in the stands and critique the other judges for classes she wasn't in or for familiar types she didn't have. Honestly, if being liked was a criterion for staying alive, she'd have died long ago."

"I'm not usually the head judge, so I avoided the critiques that Deena got," Ben said, "But even so, I noticed that she was less than respectful to other entrants. I always graded her down for it. Because it's not something that's set up to be done at Waverton, I'm not sure how much I could lower her score for being annoying, but I'd've found a way even if it got me a complaint. I think LaDona heard from Luanne every year."

"I'd tell the WBI to look at LaDona if it were up to me," Deena laughed. "She's definitely had more than one issue with Luanne. Last year Luanne made her so mad, LaDona kicked her out of the competition. That was a relief."

"Wow!" I said, listening to that. "She seemed critical, but I had no idea. I'm amazed she kept competing."

"She was good," Deena said. "If you wanted to see someone walk through the competition at one hundred percent, she was the entrant to watch. She was perfect or close enough every single time. She always placed, but not quite as high as she would have if she hadn't been so difficult and so ethically challenged."

Deena held up the water dish and headed down to the kitchen.

"Deena's head judge on this," Ben said when she left. "We're about equal in seniority but I don't mind second chair. You're third, of course, because you're new. Next year, you'll be on the list and if you volunteer to judge again, you can haggle for a higher chair if that interests you. After three years or six competitions, you get paid for judging. I'm not sure LaDona mentioned that last part."

"She didn't," I said. "She made this sound like it was a trial."

Ben moved his shoulders from side to side so that his head bopped back and forth. "You have to be really bad to get booted after the trial. She probably scared you about the whole *don't place a murderer* thing, too. It's the ethics part. There's nothing in the Waverton competition about ethics which means that LaDona is always making things up to try and push us to be more conscientious about things like that. She's tried having the entry rules and judging guidelines changed but because of the possible involvement of ordinaries, they keep the witch gossip out of this competition."

I laughed. It wasn't like an ordinary person would understand the competitions or how they worked. It was mostly using magic in conjunction with a familiar and looked almost normal. Still, we tried to avoid having them in the building and few ever found their way inside thanks to our spells. But the WBI was all about what-ifs in terms of being seen by ordinaries.

"Do you actually spell out the ethics scores in other competitions?" I asked. "Is that why we don't have them in Waverton?"

"If someone challenges a score, that challenge can become public. If it has to go on Waverton's website, then yes, the ethics could be out there where anyone could read it, though I doubt many ordinary people are breathlessly following the competition scores." Ben shrugged a bit and sat down, though his chair was turned towards the center of the room.

"So," I asked, "what happens next? I know we work out who does what, but what else?"

"We'll get comfortable with each other's familiars. I'm sure that Night Shadow has introduced herself to Mason. And Mason's probably met Bistro." Ben gestured to Deena's familiar. He was sniffing around the kennel and looked up at Ben's words, having heard his name.

I noted that Bistro had large gold eyes that matched his fur, which was some of the longest fur I had ever seen. He looked larger than I suspected he was.

"Bistro is almost as outgoing as Deena when it comes to talking to people," Ben said. "Aren't you?"

Bistro gave the tiniest kitten mew I had ever heard. It was almost laughable coming from the large cat. I decided that whatever else happened, I was going to like working with Ben and Deena.

When Deena came back, I learned the ropes. Deena sent me another document online so I could read more rules and learn more about how the judging worked.

"LaDona really ought to send this part out as well. It's not as if it's a deep secret, but she never does," Deena said. "I've trained four of you newbies since my early days, and while

LaDona has a good eye in who is judging material, she's very odd about the way she goes about things."

"Are you saying, like Ben, that I don't have to worry about placing a murderer?" I asked. It was only half in jest.

"Knowing LaDona, she'd hold that against you, but the competition rules typically state that such things can't be held against you as a judge. If you do everything else well, it's not an issue. It's not like we expect you to be a police officer. You're just judging a contest and this one doesn't even have an ethics component."

Deena shook her head as if this was a huge oversight, though from what Ben had said it had been something that had been hashed out over the years, and whoever ran things decided it was better this way than changing it.

Reaching down to rub Bistro's ears, Deena nodded. "He says that Mason works very well with them and seems a pleasant enough fellow." That made Deena smile again. If she were in my café, my sales would probably triple as people came in just to see her. She had that sort of warm and fuzzy personality.

Ben cleared his throat and we all settled in to discuss who would do what when our competition came up. We'd just worked ourselves to a natural stopping point, when Deena said she needed a break to get something to drink.

As Deena stood to leave, I heard someone out in the hallway.

"You can't be in on this, Tom," a male voice said. It sounded like Chief Spader.

I got up and went to the door. Tom Alsez was outside the conference room.

His face looked as stormy as I'd ever seen it.

"Julia had nothing to do with this murder," Tom snapped. "I don't think she even knew the victim."

My heart thundered and my stomach rolled. My hands

shook and I put one up to grab the door. My sister wasn't a murderer. The police couldn't think that, not really. She had to just be in for more questioning.

I felt someone behind me, looking over my shoulder. Ben. He had a comforting presence which was a good thing as I nearly fainted when I saw Tyson hurrying down the hallway to the conference room, probably because Julia needed a lawyer.

1 2

"Tom?" I called out when Ben had steadied me.

Tom turned from where he stood in the hallway, his eyes searching for who had said his name. It took him longer to focus on me than it should have, which told me how rattled he was. Something had gone very wrong.

"What's going on?" I asked. I walked out of the judge's room, my legs stiff with fear and my feet barely feeling the floor beneath them.

"They said the scarf belonged to Julia," Tom said, his voice nearly cracking.

"I've never seen it," I said, frowning. Although maybe I had. I mean she made scarves like that one all the time.

"Julia said it was hers when they showed her." Tom seemed perplexed as to how that could be. "She didn't know it was missing…told us where it would be in her house…but there was nothing like it there. Chief Spader is questioning her. They have to because she didn't know the scarf was missing and she should have. They're searching her home for traces of negative magic and to see what her magical signature feels like...I can't be in on the investigation... I don't know..."

Tom was reacting just as badly as I was.

"It can't be Julia. She had no reason," I said.

"Except that Luanne had complained about her quilt to the quilt judges," Tom said. "Said it didn't look hand done and they needed to avoid impropriety."

"Even so. Julia's not that competitive." I knew it was a poor argument, but I knew my sister. She didn't do this.

Tom shook his head. "We know that. But objectively... I can't think that the WBI will find anything in her home, but..."

I went over and hugged him. Two months ago, while I had liked Tom, I hadn't ever envisioned hugging him.

"Do my folks know?" I asked. I realized that with Tyson in the room, Julia had good representation. Tyson and his brother, Tim were the best attorneys in town.

"Julia didn't want me to call them," Tom said, referring to my parents.

I considered calling them right then. Julia hadn't said anything to me, but I knew she'd know Tom had talked to me. I didn't want her to get angry with him for something I had done. I needed to wait, at least for a little bit.

Julia and I were pretty close, but we had the usual sisterly fights, especially when Julia got into big sister mode. She thought I was wasting my talents working in shelters and now at the cat café. She'd have loved to see me as a vet tech or even a veterinarian. I had gone to school for that but never felt passionate about the job.

My mom understood. My dad was less than enthusiastic, though he'd come around when I got awards from the mayor for my café. Julia still seemed put out. Like she felt she had to work harder because I wasn't going to be our parents' prestigious career child. That left her working harder to fulfill that dream.

Dad wasn't a bad guy and he didn't pressure us, really. But I knew that he hoped that one of us would get a good job, a steady job. But both of his daughters had followed passions into something other than the steady work he had hoped for. I ran my own café, which had a certain amount of prestige, but it didn't offer the financial security my dad would have liked.

Julia did fabric art and worked in a fabric store that sold craft items. She also did a lot of sewing for other people, making her way as a seamstress when she needed a bit of extra. As far as I was concerned, her job was practical, but my dad didn't see it that way. I suppose if she'd gone to college and majored in business and took over managing a fabric store for a large conglomerate, he would have felt better, but she hadn't gone that way either.

It wasn't that he wasn't proud of us, but he worried.

And Julia took had taken that worry on, pushing me to go into veterinary medicine or taking on a tech job that I had been offered that didn't really interest me. I was glad I'd held out, but I'm not sure she was. She'd been nice enough to get wholesale fabric for me and sewed up blinds for the café, but she rarely asked how things were going, almost as if she were afraid I'd tell her they weren't going all that well.

Also, taking on the big sister role, she didn't approve of most of the boys or men I dated. I wasn't even sure she completely approved of Tyson, though, like me, she'd known him all her life. I mean, given that Trinity, his younger sister, was one of my best friends and had spent a huge portion of her childhood in our house, Julia knew him and his family as well as anyone. And, you'd think she'd approve, considering Tyson was an attorney and it was the sort of career our father appreciated.

Maybe it was because she was involved with Tom, a police officer, and she had some idea that there was competition.

"I wish there was something I could do," I muttered.

Tom shook his head. "I'll keep an ear out for as much as I can, but I'm not sure what they'll tell me. Probably about what Julia would tell me, I guess."

I hoped that Tom would learn more. Everyone gossiped, even police officers. And I knew that if you had the right friends you could find things out.

Tom walked back down the hallway, pacing. I stood near the door.

I heard murmurs behind me and the smell of strong coffee, almost too strong. I looked back. Deena had returned. She came out of the office and put her arms around me and led me back inside.

"I heard that was your sister," she said. "I don't know this town so I have nothing to offer. But what do you need from me?"

I nearly cried. I noticed that her water was actually coffee and I almost asked for that, but even I wouldn't stoop that low.

"I don't know," I said. "I'm in shock. I mean everyone is being questioned, but Tom said the scarf that was used to strangle Luanne came from Julia's home. And she admitted that. The WBI is apparently there now."

I wondered briefly if I could find Lina among all the fair goers but I knew that WBI witches were good at blending in when they needed to.

Deena drew me into the room a bit further and I sank into my chair while Ben watched, not saying a word.

"We were going to go over the rules but that was the only thing we had for the morning," he said. "LaDona is good about making sure the judges have plenty of time. We can skip that until afternoon."

"I think that would help me concentrate," I said.

Deena reached down to touch Bistro. Mirroring her, I reached down for Mason.

Julia wouldn't know how to do a negative spell if someone tried to teach her, Mason snapped, irritably once he learned what was going on. *You really need to find out who did kill this woman, not just for you but for your sister.*

Mason was right. I did need to figure out who did it.

"I think that a break would be good," Deena said. "How about fifteen minutes? You can slip out and make any calls you need and clear your head. Maybe get a soda or something. I know you're probably a coffee drinker, but I find that there isn't any really good coffee at the fair and no doubt you're used to the best. I'm going to go get one of the cinnamon rolls I was smelling earlier. Ben?"

Ben stood. "I'm a big fan of the scones they have here."

We did do good scones at the fair. Light and fluffier than most and they were served with a dollop of butter and jam on the side. Of course, their dollops were the size of ice cream scoops, so no one ever complained about not having enough.

I waited for my stomach to growl, but nothing happened except a minor bout of nausea. If nothing else had told me how upset I was, that did it.

I watched as Deena and Ben left the room. I bent down and talked to Mason for a minute. Then I texted Natalie and sent a similar one to Trinity.

Natalie, of course, responded before I was halfway through writing to Trinity. She was working that day, but she'd find out what she could. What she did know was that Luanne was from the Chicago area and her neighbors weren't very fond of her.

That seemed to be a running theme.

The next text said that Luanne had had an argument with another guest and the on-duty manager had had to step in. Apparently, the other guest knew Luanne from other competitions and said that they were going to make sure she didn't win.

That sounded ominous. Unfortunately, the on-duty manager was vague on the description of the guest arguing with Luanne. Just that it was a woman taller and thinner than Luanne.

Trinity wrote back. She had asked her new boyfriend Liam about it. Liam worked for Trinity's brother Tyson as an investigator. He'd been brought on when their last investigator had been murdered. I doubted that if Tyson took the case that he'd be able to say much about it, but perhaps he was easier to get information from than Tyson.

Plus, Trinity could sometimes pick up things telepathically if she were close to someone and they were thinking hard about something. I hoped that her questions would make Liam think very hard indeed. I wanted to know why the cops were looking so closely at Julia.

I mean, I understood that the scarf being hers put her in their crosshairs, but something had Tom upset and I had a feeling it was because he knew something he wasn't saying.

My phone buzzed again. Natalie.

LaRue didn't like Jujube.

I puzzled over what that meant. Then I realized that Natalie's familiar, LaRue had probably disliked Luanne's familiar, named Jujube.

That was interesting, but didn't get me any closer to who might want to murder her. Only that her familiar wasn't necessarily likable from LaRue's standpoint. I had to admit that LaRue was a particularly picky cat. She tolerated guests at the hotel and mostly stayed in Natalie's office or the front area. However, when the hotel was busy, she had a tendency to wander through the halls, getting a sense of all the guests staying in what she considered her territory.

She could be very easygoing, but LaRue wasn't interested in getting close to many people. She didn't even particularly like it when Natalie got close to people. The petite little gray and white cat could give the most disapproving looks. Natalie assured me that LaRue liked me but I wasn't completely certain she wasn't lying.

Deena bustled back inside. "You okay, dear?"

I nodded. "I texted a couple of friends. They'll make sure that if Julia needs something and can't get me that she'll be taken care of."

"I can't imagine you being related to a murderer. One of my talents is picking up on people's motivations and I see nothing dark in you. It's hard to be that light-spirited when you're around a person with darker motivations," Deena said. "And Bistro likes Mason, and your familiar picked you. It can't possibly be your sister. I hope the police realize that soon enough."

Ben walked back in just then. He nodded at both of us. "I tried listening in on the police talking. I guess the WBI hasn't found any traces of negative magic in the home, but the magical signature is close to the one used on the scarf."

"Julia's never done a negative spell in her life. Even when the kids were playing, it wasn't her thing, you know?" I said. "She can be pushy and she's naïve about certain things and doesn't think twice about picking up something belonging to someone else, though she'll return it if you tell her she took it, but she's about as divorced from negative spells as anyone I know."

Deena nodded and patted my knee. "Sometimes it takes a bit of time for things to sort themselves out."

"The canine judges are on the other side of the conference room," Ben said. "Guess they've been approached by Celia Wood as they walked through the doors."

Deena rolled her eyes and shook her head. Seeing my expression. "Celia is the favored working class canine familiar winner. She's taken first place in four other competitions and best overall once before. Two more of those and she'll be forced to retire. I think some of the canine judges are looking forward to that."

"Once the witches in the competition start recognizing you as a judge, you'll get some of this," Ben said. "Celia always comes up to the judges and reminds them of who she is and the good things they said about her last time. It's like reminding people that she was good a month ago, as if they couldn't remember, will make it easier for her to place."

"She's also suggested certain things," Deena said. "Not quite a bribe but it's possible to be taken that way. 'You know, if Kandy Karmen wins, we'll be working on such and such and I bet you'd like that.' The implication is that the judge would get a gift, maybe, but it's even more subtle than that so she avoids the impropriety of trying to bribe a judge."

"Which would definitely get her kicked out of the competition altogether," Ben added quickly. "It's that make nice thing that she does. I've even gotten it a few times because she knows I judge working feline familiars and I could be picked to be in the main ring."

Deena shook her head. "I can't believe you'd want that job! Everyone would be angry at your choices. I'm opinionated, but I like my feline fiefdom! The witches who work with me mostly know what I'm about and they know I can't be swayed. The others, well, I'd have to train them up and I don't quite have the energy. It's bad enough when I get moved up in the feline division!"

Another chuckle. Low energy was the last thing I'd have

described Deena as, but perhaps even her persistent upbeat mood wasn't as easy as she made it look.

"It raises my profile," Ben said. "They might hate me for my decisions but that doesn't mean they won't purchase my books, even if they only want to criticize everything. And reviews are good no matter how bad they are."

Deena nodded. "See, I'm a therapist and Bistro comes to work with me as a registered therapy cat, though we don't go into places. It just allows him to be in my office. I run my own business and I'm rarely gone more than half a week at a time so my clients don't get disruptions in their life. I don't need to raise my profile, as you say."

It made sense that Deena, with her easy-going manner and her ability to get a sense of people, would be a therapist. I had a feeling she was much sought after, and not just because she had Bistro. With her talent and a familiar who was good with patients, I couldn't imagine people being in better hands.

The three of us settled in to go over the rules and what they meant. As we worked, I realized how much of this was about interpretation of the written rules. Deena had notes on how things had been interpreted in other years. Ben had arguments for some of those but mostly he deferred. I had never considered rule interpretation.

As we finished up it was nearly lunchtime.

"We'll role play after lunch," Deena said. "That's always the fun part."

I smiled a little. Ben had keys and gave one to each of us. I gave Mason one last ear rub before heading out to lunch. I hoped that Trinity was at the specialty library booth so I could talk to her about Julia.

Deena locked the door behind me as I hurried out, only to run into Tyson who didn't look at all happy.

13

As we approached the outside door, I heard rain pelting the ground. Now that I was finally getting out to go grab a bite, though I had little appetite, I was going to get soaked. I was surprised to see Tyson's suit jacket was dry. Only then did I notice he carried a dripping umbrella.

While he didn't look happy, that turned to surprise and then a smile when he saw me. That melted my insides. His molded clay good looks always did that. A few strands of dark hair hung out of place over his forehead and I had to practically hold my hand against my belly to keep from pushing into place.

Ben hadn't even noticed Tyson and when he opened the outside door, I got a whiff of the fresh rain and the assorted smells of the food dome.

"You heard about Julia?" Tyson asked.

"I was here all morning. Tom was pretty upset," I said. "She hasn't been arrested yet, has she?"

Tyson frowned and looked down.

"She has?!" I practically screamed.

"Look, I can't talk about it because she's a client, but the arrest is public record and she's your sister. Your folks were both called."

I nodded. Not that they could do anything, really. Tyson was likely the only one who could.

"Why aren't you there?" I asked.

"They're processing her. I'm told official questioning will begin later this afternoon. Julia knows not to say a word without me, so they'll definitely call when they want to chat with her."

"I can't believe it," I said. "Julia doesn't do negative magic. I know that Ben heard that they found some similarities in her magical signature, but it's not her."

"Signatures aren't everything," Tyson said. "Just a similarity isn't enough." He stopped himself from saying more. I had a feeling Julia admitting that the scarf belonged to her was a huge reason she was arrested.

"How did they know the scarf was hers?" I asked.

"Shannon Coombs said it looked like Julia's work. The two have been in competitions against each other before. Add that to the fact that a bunch of people overheard Luanne practically screaming at Julia..." Tyson trailed off. "I should go before I tell you something that you probably don't already know. There are too many confidential things I can't say."

He turned away from me. I grabbed his hand and squeezed it before he was out of reach. He squeezed mine back. This was going to be difficult. Julia would be foremost on my mind and he probably had things that couldn't be said about her case, many of which might comfort me.

I breathed out and let him go. I really wasn't hungry, but I knew I needed food. Still, it wouldn't hurt to talk to Trinity first.

I decided it would be faster to go out the other side of the competition building so I turned around and hurried in that direction. I passed a couple of other people who were probably judges, heading in the direction of the food dome. I passed several other offices that were closed and a few with doors left open and familiars waiting. In one, I saw three ferrets with their kennels all pushed together so they could press noses against them.

I was surprised that all the judges for that category had ferrets. Usually, the exotics had a variety of familiars.

Soon enough, I was at the other door, noting the rain. I wasn't far from a side door to the food and floral building. It was a shorter run than trying to go around. I'd get wet enough as it was. I'd been in such a hurry earlier that I'd forgotten an umbrella. I was going to pay for it now.

I ran across the hard-packed earth, which was starting to turn to mud, but at least I was going away from where others were heading and it wasn't quite so messy. Even so, my tidy black and white cross-trainers would probably be filthy.

Inside, I noticed that judges were placing ribbons on some of the food as I cut through the aisles. The sawdust in there stayed dry and it wasn't too messy. The rain drummed against the roof of the building and it echoed loudly enough that I couldn't hear the low music they played.

Tables held lines of jams and jellies. I paused before one that had a blue ribbon noting it was strawberry and the spell on it was to ease irritability. It was too bad they weren't giving out samples so I could try it.

I brushed past a few people who were reading the labels on what others had entered. When I'd been younger and my sister was entering the first few times, she would drag my mom and me through the craft buildings and read everything, getting a good idea of what other people had done and what the competition was. Her work had always been adult level even when she was a teenager. She hadn't always placed, but she got some great comments.

I pushed back thoughts of Julia and wove my way through a side aisle so that I could get across the building. Soon enough I was at a door on the far side. No one was coming in that way. I noticed that a couple of people looked out the door across the way and then turned. I didn't blame them.

Puddles of water stood between the two buildings. I backed up and headed for another door. Fortunately, there were several along the long sides of the building.

Looking out at the next one, I noticed the mud that I'd worried about, but not nearly as many puddles. I hurried out, feeling my feet stick in the softened dirt. I sighed thinking about my poor shoes. At least they weren't my good dress shoes.

At the next building, I did my best to wipe them off on the sawdust that covered the dirt inside, but it wasn't much help. No wonder the fair personnel kept dirt floors in the buildings and just tossed out fresh sawdust. On rainy days the mud would get everywhere.

I hurried inside, belatedly realizing this was the building that Luanne had died in. It made my stomach feel funny and the knots that had been tightening down in my intestines got worse as I made my way through the quilts. I barely looked at the artwork hanging around me. I paid attention only to the people who were talking with each other so that I could avoid running into them.

The walk reminded me of the sort that happens in night-mares. I kept walking, but I never got closer to my goal. At least some shadowy monster wasn't chasing me, at least not that I knew of. Of course, if it was a nightmare, maybe I'd wake up to Mason's warmth against my cold feet on a morning where Julia hadn't been arrested for murder.

I arrived at a side door soon after I had that thought. Not likely to be a dream then. I sighed. No puddles, but plenty of churned-up mud. I hurried out, passing a couple of men sharing a wide blue umbrella.

My hair lay plastered down around my face by the time I got to the next building. I'd been wet before. Now I was soaked. I didn't even try to clean off my shoes. I just hurried through the building towards the specialty library booth.

The noise level was louder in the vendor building. The vendors were all there to answer questions and sell products so it wasn't just people talking to each other, but people talking to those who wanted to educate and perhaps sell items. The rain had ceased to drum quite as quickly.

I smiled at a few vendors who met my eye. Others were too busy talking to people, though one woman was pointedly looking away from the crowds. I didn't man vendor booths, but I knew in the café that making eye contact was important.

I crossed an aisle and then turned towards the back of the building to the specialty library's large booth. Trinity was there, of course, but she had a chair this time. A few kids were talking to her, the adult shepherding them standing back a few inches from the table. They finished about the time I arrived.

"Have you learned anything?" I whispered to Trinity.

"Liam isn't talking because he's been hired to look into things by Tyson," Trinity said. "I guess that means that Julia has officially hired them."

"She's been arrested," I said. "Who else would she hire? Tom was about fit to be tied. And you know my sister. If anything, she'd report one of us for doing a small negative magic spell. She wouldn't be dabbling in it."

"I did do some reading between people," Trinity whispered. "A similar magical signature doesn't mean much in the courts. Yes, it's enough to cast suspicion and the police need to follow up, but the evidence is thin. It's like finding a drop of blood with a matching blood type. I mean, maybe a bit more than that, but not much. It's not unique."

I sort of knew that, but didn't know how it worked for courts.

"I heard she told them the scarf was hers. That's both good and bad. It's bad because this gives cause to arrest her, particularly given the magical signature. It's like saying, yes I was at the scene and they match your blood type. It's not a big leap, but it's all circumstantial," Trinity went on.

"And it's good how?" I asked.

"It shows she didn't think she had anything to hide," Trinity said. "I'm sure Tyson isn't thrilled now, but it would have been harder to work with a jury and build alternate theories if Julia hadn't said, yes I recognize that scarf. I think it's mine."

I nodded. I got what she was saying. Julia's actions weren't the actions of a criminal trying to hide something. Of course, they could be considered the actions of a criminal who was proud of their crime, too. It depended upon how the jury saw it.

"We really need to find out who did this," I said. "I heard that Olivia, who competes with her horse, has a cousin that quilts, too. I guess she's the one who said the scarf looked like something Julia might make."

"What's her name?"

"Shannon Coombs," I told her about Olivia, too, just in case. The two might have worked together. While I'd been inclined to believe Olivia the day before, now I was wondering if her act was too good to be true.

"Jade!"

I turned at the sound of the male voice. Mark Wells. He and his husband bred Maine Coon familiars. Mark was tall and broad with curly blonde hair. Today he was dressed in blue jeans pressed to a crease on the legs and a button-down plaid shirt. He wasn't wearing a jacket.

"Mark. How are you?" I asked.

"I'm doing well," he said. "And I'll be seeing you in the ring."

"I saw your name on the list," I said.

"I hope you'll think of me favorably. Morgenstern helps out with gaming ideas and I think we work well together. We've never placed before, but you never know, the sixth time might be the charm, right?" Mark said. He laughed a little. I knew that he programmed computer games. I did not know that his familiar came up with ideas, though I wasn't sure what kind he might think of. Catching mice?

"Maybe," I said, still smiling. I felt weird having the conversation knowing that I would be one of the reasons he did or didn't place this year.

"At least I won't be up against Luanne," he said. "She always placed. It feels like space has opened up for those of us who were always honorable mentions. Not that I'm glad she's dead or anything." Mark added that last hurriedly.

"It is too bad what happened to her. I've heard that a lot of people didn't like her," I said.

"I'd hate to speak ill of the dead," Mark said. Then he lowered his voice. "I didn't much like her. She said Morgenstern was too fat and should be disqualified."

Morgenstern was a huge Maine Coon cat that had come from one of Mark's breeder queens. His long gray and black fur shimmered in the right light when Mark took photos of the two of them together. Both always looked contented. I followed the cattery on Facebook, so his photos often came up on my timeline.

"That's rude," I said. I hadn't read anything in the rules, nor had we gone over anything that suggested the weight or size of the cat should disqualify him or her. Part of the judging was looking at the feline's body which should be proportional and of a "good weight" which was determined by the judge. A fat cat might get marked down a bit but there was no reason for it to be disqualified.

I didn't say any of that to Mark.

"I know, right? Morgenstern is a Maine Coon. They're supposed to be big. And he's not fat, not really." Mark sighed. "Of course, people say I'm fat too and they're right, but at least I'm smart, rich, and a decent human being."

I laughed when he did. He was right. There were certainly worse things to be than being fat.

I was lucky that I only had to watch my weight a bit. My mom remained thin, though my dad started putting on weight as he got older. I breathed into his comment, hoping that when I got older, and maybe had kids, and put on some extra pounds I could let that go as easily as Mark did.

Mark slipped off into a crowd of people. Trinity had started talking to an older gentleman and then moved on to a woman. I waited. Finally, she was finished.

"I'll keep you posted on what I find. Have you texted this information to Natalie? Shannon might be staying at the hotel."

"If Shannon's related to Olivia, maybe she's not. Horse people," I said. Horse owners often had an RV or a camper of some sort so they could stay close to the horse stables. I'd seen a couple out in the parking lot.

"Worth a try," Trinity said.

I nodded and made to head back. Someone was selling specialty fudge and I purchased a hunk of that. I didn't really want it, but I probably needed to eat something before the day finished and I didn't really have much time to run over to the food dome. So this would be lunch.

It melted nicely in my mouth. I was reminded of how rich

fudge was with its thick chocolate flavor. I had gotten a piece with pecans and the crunch of those made a lovely contrast to the smoothness of the rest. Of course, now I needed water.

I hurried back through the buildings, hoping to get back to the competition building before my lips glued themselves together.

I was nearly at the kitchen and planning to find a mug when I ran into Tom Alsez and he looked pretty forlorn. At least I could drink water and talk at the same time.

Tom wasn't much taller than I was. I mean, most people are because I'm rather short, but Tom was only half a head taller, maybe. He had one of those stoic faces that made you believe he could handle anything. It's a good look for a cop. Unfortunately, he wasn't looking stoic at all today.

"What is it?" I asked as I gestured for him to follow me into the little kitchen. As I had remembered, there were a bunch of mugs in there. I grabbed one and filled it with the filtered water that came out of the sink. I'd have liked cooler water, but this would do.

"Julia is still being questioned," Tom said. "And there are a few of the cops who really think she did it. They're ready to close the book, no matter what I tell them."

"It's not everyone, though, is it?" I asked. I couldn't believe the whole Waverton police department would believe my sister was a murderer.

Tom shook his head. "No, fortunately. But it's hard to hear them talk about her like she really could have done this.

It's basic circumstantial evidence. Someone saw the scarf in her house and took it and then used it to kill someone."

"Where was the scarf, do you know?"

"Julia always kept everything on the coat tree by the door."

I pictured my sister's house. She had a beautiful free-standing bench with coat hooks above it near her door. Hand-painted in pale blue and white. It looked old-fashioned, all that hand-painting, and suited her. She'd stenciled some cats on it. My whole family adored cats.

Both summer and winter coats were there along with scarves. Gloves went inside the bench which opened for storage. Knit hats did too, though she had a place for fancier hats that couldn't easily be folded. Julia loved dressing up in hats of any sort.

The scarf would have been there, near the door, easy to grab. Most people in Waverton locked their doors, but it wasn't a big deal if someone forgot. No one double or triple checked doors if they forgot. Of course, most witches had spells in place to let them know who would have come in. And they could always spell to see who had been inside.

"Did the police check to see if anyone came in while Julia was gone?" I asked.

"The WBI tried," Tom said. "It's sort of like everything is blank for a few hours, which lends credence to the fact that someone came in. Of course, Julia could have been the one who wiped the timeframe. It would be the smart thing to do to keep people from believing she'd kill someone."

It made sense.

"Why would someone want to frame my sister?" I wondered out loud.

"I think she was convenient," Tom said. "She lived in the area. She had something that would work as a murder weapon, and Luanne had been heard loudly criticizing the quilt Julia put in the show. I've heard that someone over-heard Luanne talking to Julia and the two had words."

The fact that Julia was local would have meant that it was easier to plant clues in her home to lead the police and WBI to where they needed to go. The real murderer, who clearly knew something about negative magic, would have wanted someone with a magical signature similar to their own.

"The murderer could also have read Julia's magical signature on the quilt and realized it was similar enough to their own to make it appear that Julia was the murderer," I said.

Tom nodded. "I thought that, too. I scanned several of the quilts and two others are close matches to Julia's magical signature. One is the horse quilt a few rows down and the other is a baby quilt. Neither of the crafters lives locally, though."

The horse quilt, though, had been done by Shannon Coombs and she had multiple reasons to want Luanne dead.

"I heard that Luanne criticized Shannon Coombs too. She's the one who made the horse quilt. And Shannon's cousin, Olivia is in the equine working class competition and is one of the entrants favored to place."

"Maybe I should look into this woman," Tom said thoughtfully.

"Don't get in trouble for it," I said. "If they want you off the case, they want you off the case. If you can let someone working it know what you know…"

Tom nodded, but he turned and walked away quickly, a lighter step than earlier. I worried that Chief Spader would learn what he was doing and Tom would lose his job. He was a good cop and clearly, he adored my sister.

I sighed. I refilled the mug with water. Deena bustled in as I was doing that.

"No caffeine for lunch?" she asked. "You're good."

"I ended up talking to a friend at lunch and didn't even

get over to the food dome." I sighed, looking at the water. Some coffee would be good but the pot in the kitchen was empty and I had a feeling that it didn't exactly brew a cup that would please me.

"I understand you're upset, but you can't forget to eat. Particularly not when we're up as judges. The stress of being out there can make you feel disoriented and light-headed."

"It's not like me to skip a meal." I gave her a smile.

"Besides, you pick up all sorts of gossip at the food dome. I heard that Olivia Coombs's cousin Shannon has quite a vendetta against Luanne. Luanne has criticized her quilts in any number of competitions. There are rumors that in the competition we had in Washington state last year that Luanne got Shannon's quilt disqualified and that's why neither Shannon nor Olivia competed there. Of course, Washington is a bit out of their travel zone so it could be that," Deena said.

"You overheard all of that?" I asked.

"I didn't 'overhear'," Deena said, "I talked. And Shannon and Olivia aren't the only ones. Celia who has Kandy Karmen cannot stand Luanne. That one is more personal. Luanne swore that Kandy Karmen chased her familiar once at the behest of Celia, but who knows? Dogs play and Luanne and Jujube aren't exactly known for their sense of humor."

It didn't sound like it. I sort of felt bad for Luanne's familiar. "Did Luanne have any family to take Jujube in?" I asked.

"You know, I don't know," Deena said. "I mean, I know she has family but she wasn't married. I don't know if they're cat people or not. I suppose if they aren't, then Jujube'll come to you?"

"Not automatically. A witch has to actually know about the café. Most witch communities know about the shelter here in Waverton, though, and they know about me. I have more space to help a familiar who's lost their witch suddenly come to terms with the change before allowing them to be adopted."

"I ought to go over there once we've finished judging. I've heard of cat cafes, but never seen one. And to think all your felines are familiars!" Deena giggled and grabbed a soda from the refrigerator.

"I brought extras," she said. "I am a caffeine addict. Take one. It'll perk you up if you didn't eat."

I took one of her Diet Cokes, though I prefer the regular kind, and headed down the hallway where we met Ben.

"Looked like you were having a good lunch," Ben said to Deena as she joined us.

"I talked to everyone," Deena said.

"I didn't talk to everyone, but I did talk to the WBI witch," Ben said. "She sought me out."

I glanced at him, wondering what the WBI wanted.

"She told me they were thinking of postponing our competition or even canceling it in case it wasn't about the crafts but about the familiars," Ben continued. "She asked me about the entrants and what I knew."

"We aren't going to cancel," Deena said. "LaDona would have a fit."

"I referred her there, but she was interested in me. Actually, I think she was interested in Jade. She named you a couple of times specifically." Ben nodded at me.

My stomach twisted again. At the rate it was going my stomach would be so knotted I'd never be able to eat again. A felt a slight headache creeping up on the back of my neck and I reached up to rub the area.

"Why's she interested in Jade?" Deena demanded. I had to love her for the fact that she sounded like a mother bear protecting her young, though she wasn't anywhere near old enough to be my mother.

"I think she's more interested in Jade's sister," Ben said.

"But I didn't get the sense that she believed your sister did anything."

The knots in my stomach released a little.

"Thank heavens someone doesn't believe it," I said.

"Let's hope that the local police believe that," Deena reminded me. Which twisted my stomach all back up but now I had some hope that someone, somewhere believed Julia was innocent.

"Why me?" I asked.

Ben shrugged. "I couldn't really get a read on her. She was like a ghost. Even the sense that she wasn't trying to pin something on your sister may have been something she wanted me to infer so I'd talk to her a bit more."

That sank my stomach back into the macramé knots it had been in before. I sighed. So much for help from the WBI.

15

It was late afternoon when we finished up role-playing for the competition. Deena suggested we get together for a few hours tomorrow to go over our roles one more time, but she felt good about things. I felt okay. I'd be mostly watching the others work with the entrants. My job would be to indicate when people needed to bring their cats to the judges. I could do that.

Finished for the day, I packed up Mason and got out of there. I figured I'd go to the hotel and talk to Natalie after I dropped him off.

"The café closes in an hour and a half," I told him as we left. "Do you want to be dropped off there or at the apartment?"

The apartment. I found the day tiring, talking to Bistro all day. That cat talks as much as his owner, only I don't appreciate his enthusiasm the way you do hers, Mason said.

So I headed home. I mean, home was over the café so I'd head to the same place anyway, but this way I could just go upstairs. And probably call my mom and see how she and my dad were doing with my sister being under arrest and all. My folks had been really upset when Trinity had been arrested. I couldn't imagine how they were feeling now that it was Julia.

It didn't take too long to get back to town. The fairgrounds are just outside of town, on the southwest side.

Downtown was fairly quiet. I noticed that there was a parking place in front of the specialty library, which almost never happens. It's a popular place around here. Of course, seeing it specializes in all things familiar and we are the familiar capital, that's not a huge surprise.

I parked behind my building in my reserved place and took Mason's carrier out of the car. I left the blanket and his extra dishes and the toys I brought for him. Not that he played with them. He'd mostly looked like he'd been sleeping except when he'd wash a paw.

I climbed the exterior stairs and set him down on the landing. He'd started moving around, eager to get out. Normally, when it's not too hot or too wet, I let him follow me out the door on his own rather than have him in a carrier. Shifting his weight was his way of letting me know he wasn't pleased.

Inside, my apartment was warm and cozy. Because it's right above the coffee shop, it always stays warm and cozy. In the summer it can get a bit too warm, but I have air conditioning which I probably run too much. In the winter, though, it's perfect even if I don't set the heat very high. The coffee shop takes care of that. One less personal bill for me.

I do well with the café, but I'm not getting rich.

I immediately let Mason out and he jogged over to his dish in the kitchen, glaring at me upon finding it empty. I didn't have a clue when he expected me to have filled it.

I got him a snack seeing he hadn't had anything to eat all day and let him settle in. I curled up on my sofa, running my hands over the blue and green afghan that covered the back, and called my mom.

"Hey, Mom!" I said, trying to be bright.

"Jade." Just my name. No greeting or how are you.

"What have you heard?" I asked.

"I got a call that Julia had been arrested, but nothing else. Tom hasn't even contacted us, though I've left him several messages," Mom said.

"He's off the case. You know. The relationship and all. The police don't want any hint of impropriety."

"I figured that, but he could at least call. He's practically part of the family." Mom sounded put out that she'd been overlooked.

"He probably feels like he doesn't have anything to say," I said.

"Of all the people…" Mom trailed off. I heard a sniff and knew she was crying.

"It'll work out. It did for Trinity." Hopefully, reminding her of Trinity's arrest, which wasn't exactly the arrest we'd thought. The Waverton police and the WBI were using her arrest as a way to draw out the real murderer. Still, all of us had believed the police thought she'd murdered her boss.

"But this isn't like that," Mom said. "I had hoped…but if they're not allowing Tom to work the case, you know they think there's something there."

"It's all circumstantial. Julia admitted the scarf that was used to murder the woman looked like hers. She keeps it by her door. Someone did a time-look-erase spell on her house, too." A witch could use a spell to cover their tracks on a magically guarded home or business. How well it worked depended upon the actual protection spell. Like most homes, Julia's wasn't a high-level spell and I suspect she hadn't updated it since she'd moved in.

"That should tell the police something." Mom humphed.

"It could also mean that Julia was trying to make it look like she didn't do it," I said.

Mom started to interrupt.

"I'm not saying that's what happened. It's just what the police might argue. It's up to Tyson to make sure that argument doesn't fly. I'm not sure Julia even thinks like that." I tried to talk quickly enough to calm my mother before she started in on one of her worried rants, but I also had to pick my words carefully. Julia and I had a certain amount of sibling rivalry around who was smarter and I didn't want my mom to think I thought my sister was dumb.

"That's right. She's not devious," Mom agreed. I wasn't sure, but it sounded like she put the least little bit of emphasis on "she's" which made me wonder if Mom thought I was devious. Between me and Julia, though, I probably was.

"The magical signature on the negative magic on the scarf was similar to Julia's, too," I said. "Again, that's all circumstantial, like finding a piece of brown hair that doesn't have a root to take DNA from at a crime scene."

I heard Mom blow her nose on the other end. "It almost seems as if she's being set up. I just can't see who would do that."

"Whoever killed this woman needed someone else to pin it on." I then told my mother about Shannon and Olivia.

"I'll start asking around. I mean, if they did do something like this, they shouldn't get away with it. I'll make sure everyone is trying to find the answers." Mom seemed certain that Shannon and Olivia had to have been the murderers.

"There's also the possibility that it was someone who wanted to make it look like a crafter so we'd forget that Luanne was favored to win the feline working class," I said. "Another witch with a working familiar could have done it."

"You mean you could be judging a murderer?!" That was practically a scream.

"I doubt they'll pull out an ax and kill all the judges in front of everyone," I said drily.

Mom was not amused.

The discussion went down from there. But she did seem hooked on Olivia and Shannon and would definitely be mentioning their names to Tyson. I figured he already knew, but in case he didn't, Mom would take care of things.

I sighed. Mason licked his chops watching me as I glared at the ceiling trying to figure out what to do next. Then he washed a paw and his face before leaping on my lap.

I think Tyson will take care of things for Julia, Mason assured me.

"I'm just worried about her. And Mom is so upset." I rubbed my hands in his fur.

If they asked me, I would tell them that Julia has no stink of negative magic on her. Familiars can smell it, you know. The WBI really ought to have a familiar who can do that. Mason curled up, moving his butt at an angle to let me pet him in a particularly satisfying place near his hip.

The WBI missed nothing, or at least that's how I thought of them. They always seemed one step ahead. They had to have witches or familiars who could sniff out negative magic. Julia wouldn't have any on her and then she'd be let go. Of course, the WBI also took their sweet time before getting around to anything or letting anyone know. I doubted the Waverton police had seen the original statement I had given to Lina right after the murder.

"It'd be nice if the WBI wasn't always so secretive," I said, rubbing Mason's ears making him purr contentedly. .

You just don't like it because you can't pry out their secrets.

I eyed my cat. Sometimes he got the two of us mixed up in our motivations. I had a feeling that not being able to pry out secrets was more his annoyance than mine, though I did admit that I was rather nosy. Perhaps that's why he had chosen me.

Just then, the phone rang. I looked at the caller ID. Tyson. I hurried to pick it up, wondering what he had to say.

16

Tyson and I had only been dating a couple of months and we'd been taking things very slowly. Both of us knew this had the potential to be something serious. He was Trinity's older brother so I'd known him all my life. I'd had a crush on him in high school. While I'd dated other men, I'd been between boyfriends when I set up my business. I'd spent years working long hours, too busy to think about dating.

Just about the time my business had settled into a rhythm where I could manage to start dating again, Trinity had been arrested and Tyson had reappeared in my life.

It hadn't been a smooth beginning, requiring Mason to step in and force us to sit down and chat with each other, but we'd traversed those bumps and now had a reasonably steady relationship.

I answered the phone.

"I know we were planning dinner, but I'll be working," Tyson said. "The police move slowly here."

I wasn't surprised to get that call in the least. Tyson's job was important to him. So was my café and time was something we'd need to work out between us as we moved our relationship along. I mean, if we did stay together, did I want someone who was always putting me off when I had time off? It was certainly possible that his time off only came about when I had to put in extra time at the café. That could make seeing each other more difficult.

More precious, too, but you never knew.

"I'd rather you work to get Julia home than go to dinner," I said. I meant that, too. This time.

"I know," Tyson said. He hesitated like he wanted to say more.

"Mom is really upset," I told him. He knew my parents. After all, if you grow up in a small town, everyone has at least a passing acquaintance with everyone else.

"Tom's really upset because he's off the case," Tyson said. "Someone leaked to him about the Coombs. He got in a bit of trouble for talking to them."

"I've heard their names mentioned all over the fair," I said.

"Leave this to the police." Tyson's words were an order. "You have no business going around trying to figure out who did this. No more than Tom. Your ideas might get him in even more trouble at his job. He'll be on traffic duty at least until this is over."

"You know, I'm not the only one talking. Deena talked to a bunch of people at lunch. She told me when she got back to the competition building. She did it because she knows Julia is my sister. I've heard whispers. People were talking even before Julia was arrested. And it's not like there weren't plenty of reasons to dislike Luanne. She was probably even on the WBI's radar because of her questionable ethics."

"Not a reason to die," Tyson said. "And if someone is willing to kill because they can't take criticism of their crafts or they're so intent upon winning a competition, you definitely need to keep to yourself. They won't hesitate to murder someone they think is a bit too nosey."

I agreed with that. Not that I was going to listen.

Even Mason gave me a narrow-eyed look when I hung up.

"You'd keep doing what you wanted to, you know," I told him.

I'm a cat which means my thought process is far superior. Mason washed a small part of his side before standing and stretching. I moved the wrong way and he leaped to the floor.

That might have been Mason's way of saying he worried about me, although I had to admit he was often clearer than that.

I picked up my cell phone, put it down, and then picked it up again. I needed to talk to someone. Trinity would still be busy at the fair. She was working overtime to put in hours at the table. Natalie might be working at the hotel, but she might be able to make time to chat with me.

I called rather than texting.

"I haven't found anything," Natalie said upon greeting. "The Coombses aren't staying here. I did talk to a woman named Celia. At first, she seemed annoying, but I've come to quite like her."

"What did she say?" I asked.

"She has problems with Shannon and Olivia. I guess Olivia doesn't like her and she thinks it's because she's worried Celia will place in front of her. According to Celia, Olivia would do anything to win. That nice big speech about wanting to learn to improve her abilities with her familiar is a bunch of crock."

"That wasn't the impression I got," I said. Of course, unlike witches like Deena, I didn't have a sense of people. I mean, I had the same gut reactions all people did. Sometimes

I was right but other times I was way off base. And I never knew when I was going to be right or wrong.

"I thought she was too good to be true," Natalie said. "Celia also doesn't like Shannon because she does everything she can to try and help her sister cheat the system. That quilt, for instance, the one that has the horses and is on display at the fair? Well, that was originally made for Olivia to help her bond more closely with her horse. That's why it's a horse. Luanne didn't like it because Olivia had been sleeping under that blanket at a previous competition to give herself an edge."

"I don't think that there's anything in the competition rules about not using magical items in your room," I said.

"There's not, but Celia says it's kind of unethical."

"Does Celia compete in Equestrian Working Class?" I asked. "Or another working class?"

"She's in Canine Working Class with her dog Kandy Karmen," Natalie said. "You really ought to meet her. She and her familiar are very good together. They're at the hotel. Like I said, I was sort of asking around a bit here and there and she volunteered. After she got over her snootiness we ended up having coffee in the lobby and talking."

The name snapped me back to my conversation with Deena. Celia was good at flattery and working the edges of appropriateness. This kind of flattery would work well with Natalie. Natalie is smart and she is beautiful and bossy, but that combination makes her susceptible to believing people who say *yes* just to make nice with her.

"I've heard from the judges—and you can't repeat this— that Celia is sort of bordering ethical too, in the way she talks to judges. I guess she almost promises bribes."

"Celia seems to have a way about her that could be taken that way, but I think she's just being nice. She's not very polished, if you know what I mean."

And clearly opinionated. I made a noise of agreement and Natalie continued telling me what she thought.

"I hope Trinity can find some more information on Shannon and Olivia. It'd be much easier to plan to murder someone, particularly in the craft room, if you were either involved with the crafts or if you had assistance, don't you think? One of them could have been sniffing out who had a magical signature similar to theirs and the other could have been stealing or covering for the absence of their cousin."

The latter part of Natalie's idea resonated. If you were going to murder someone, it was always good to have an alibi. Having someone you could trust to offer it was ideal.

As for sniffing out similar magical signatures, not all witches could do that. Those that could were often in demand by the WBI. Spells were helpful but they'd leave a trace.

If the scarf had been stolen more than a day before the murder, there would be few magical traces of another witch. If the WBI had picked up a signature on the time-lock-erase on Julia's protection spell, another magical signature would have stood out against Julia's own.

I sighed. Dad had been so proud when she'd built in that image capture into her spell. He'd even had her add that to the one in the house. Most protection spells just offered a warning. Some were linked directly to the witch who set them, though blood relatives could often overcome those. Others just warned when something was wrong in a space, which is what most business owners used because it didn't really matter to the owner if it was an intruder or a fire.

Homeowners typically had spells similar to businesses, though businesses generally kept theirs up more than residences. Having an image capture took more magic and most people, particularly in a town like Waverton, didn't feel it was necessary. I had heard that the witch enclaves in places like Chicago would often hire someone to do that kind of spell if they didn't have the ability themselves.

Julia had learned that because she'd thought that someday, if her fabric art took off, she'd move out of Waverton and might need it.

I really needed to find out who was framing her.

Mason and I turned in early after a light dinner. I still didn't have much of an appetite, so maybe it was good that Tyson would be working late. I wouldn't have been able to do a meal justice no matter where he might have taken me.

The next morning, I got ready and packed up Mason to head back to the fair. We had another day of role-playing to be sure we all worked together smoothly. If Deena or Ben had gotten word from LaDona that the WBI was forcing us to delay our competition or even cancel it, they'd let me know. At worst, I'd have packed up Mason for a day at the fair for no reason.

I'd like to see the fair, Mason said as I pushed him into the carrier. Some witches had familiars that would walk right in. Mason prefers to think he can do things on his own and has to be persuaded to go into the carrier.

"Even on a leash, I'm not sure what you'd see," I said. "Horses and goats and some sheep and even pigs. And then there are the craft booths. I suppose the vendors would fuss over you at the vendor building."

As well they should. I was thinking about the food dome, though.

"They don't have litter boxes at the fair except for the entrants," I said. "You had that tiny one in the kennel in the building."

Mason sniffed a bit and washed his side as I zipped up the opening to his blue and black soft-sided carrier. I picked him up along with my purse and left the apartment.

The day was cool, but there were fewer clouds than the day before. My shoes probably wouldn't come home any dirtier than they already were. When I had to actually judge, I'd need to bring a second pair. I was thinking of even bringing a second outfit, just in case.

I'd missed rush hour, such as it was. Waverton may be small but quite a few people worked outside of town. Roads out of town could get busy in the morning. Not like big city busy or anything, but as I didn't commute, it would be more traffic than I was used to.

With the sun shining down on the red, orange, and yellow leaves and the dark green of the grass, the day was gorgeous. A perfect Kentucky day. I drove by farms with old dry-laid limestone fencing. Most had black split-rail fences just beyond. Trees lined the edges of the farms and sometimes a stately old tulip poplar, leaves half dropped, would draw the eye to where it shaded part of a field.

I passed the old tobacco farm with the creosote black angled A-line roof in the distance. Then it was back to the horse farms with the long low barns so comfortable looking I sometimes longed to move in.

I turned off towards the fair, passing a field with three horses out grazing. One glanced up at me, perhaps wondering if I was someone it knew. I didn't recognize the horse as belonging to any of my friends in town. As I thought that, the horse turned away from my car and went back to the grass.

I found a good parking spot near the judge's entrance. I grabbed my lanyard with my ID from my purse and then got Mason from the back. I picked up Mason's other stuff and headed in. I figured if nothing else this was good practice for carrying around a baby and assorted products required for away from home care.

I heard voices coming from other parts of the building as soon as I walked in the door. For a moment I felt as though I was late, but then realized it was only two people talking.

"I don't know if I can be fair to Olivia," the first voice said. The voice was low enough in range that it could have belonged to either a man or woman.

"Then maybe you need to recuse yourself instead of demanding she be disqualified," the other voice said. This one was definitely female.

"She's implicated in a murder." First voice, more raised than before. I walked slowly, though I didn't purposely try to be quiet.

"Someone else was arrested for it, a disgruntled crafter. You can't decide you know more than the police."

Julia wasn't actually a disgruntled crafter, nor was she was a murderer. I wanted to go flying down the hall and confront them, but knew I'd learn more walking more slowly and listening in.

"I'm not giving up my judging spot. And Olivia needs to toe the line."

"She does. She follows the rules, and we're lucky for that. She's the favorite in our group and is more ethical than half the people in the canine or feline working groups."

I came around the slight curve of the hallway. The first woman saw me and clamped her lips together. I looked at her, smiled, and said good morning.

While both responded pleasantly, they eyed me suspiciously as if they worried I might have overheard them.

They were standing just outside the office my team had been assigned. Deena had locked up the night before, but someone had opened the door. I glanced in. Ben wasn't there. I stepped in and put Mason in his kennel. Neither Bistro nor Night Shadow were in their kennels yet. Whoever opened the building for the fair must have opened up the judging offices.

Once Mason was settled, I went out to the kitchen and got him some water. I didn't see the other two women, though I did notice the shadow of a newly closed door down the hall a bit. Perhaps they'd been to the kitchen and were returning. They wouldn't necessarily have anything with them. Their equine familiars would be out in the barn.

It made me thankful to have a familiar like Mason that I could take places.

By the time I returned to the office, Deena was getting Bistro settled.

"Good morning," she said. "I'm surprised Ben isn't here. Usually he's an early bird."

"Maybe he had something to attend to?" I suggested.

"Not like him at all." Deena frowned and looked over at the kennel. She reached into Bistro and half-closed her eyes. Bistro and Night Shadow would have worked together before. Chances were Bistro could ask Night Shadow what was going on.

"Oh dear," Deena said.

"What?" Sudden fear gripped me. I liked Ben and didn't want him to come to harm.

"Someone was murdered in the hotel. Ben was asked to wait until the police could question him. Night Shadow is getting very antsy. Ben was leaving when the police stopped him."

I picked up my phone to check for texts from Natalie. She had to know what was going on.

Finding none, I sent her a quick note.

My phone dinged moments later with a response.

Dad managing police. I'm managing guests. Not happy.

Which was about as minimal of a response as I'd ever gotten from Natalie. I wasn't sure if she wasn't happy about her dad being there or if the guests weren't happy. Probably both. Natalie liked being in charge and if her dad were talking to the police and helping out, then Natalie had been cut off from a source of information.

"I wonder who it was," I said frowning at my phone. Too bad Natalie didn't have a name.

Deena continued kneeling down by Bistro, rubbing his back. She half-closed her eyes again for a moment and waited. I was surprised she went through the process of having to concentrate so hard while communicating with her familiar. Beginners did that, but those with experience working with their familiar didn't usually have to.

It took a few moments to get a response from Night Shadow.

"Night Shadow wasn't sure about the name, but thought it sounded like Shannon Coombs," Deena said.

"You mean like Shannon the crafter who was related to Olivia?" I said. My heart sank. If Shannon had been killed, then she probably wasn't Luanne's murderer. Olivia might have done it on her own, but I had a hard enough time imagining her as a murderer in the first place. It was nearly impossible to consider her when her own relative was involved.

"Oh my," Deena said. "This isn't good for your sister, is it?"

"Well, she couldn't have murdered Shannon. She was in

jail, but it does mean that Shannon wasn't the crafter who did it instead of her."

"That's right. I hate to think about what Olivia is going through. I rather like her, though I haven't had a ton of interactions. My impression is that the people who love her, *love* her and those that think she's a phony, hate her. Most of those who think she's a phony have lost competitions to her," Deena said, nodding. "I didn't know Shannon really. In fact, until you mentioned it, I had forgotten they were related."

I knelt and petted Mason. He'd pick up what I knew and maybe come up with something while I worked. Besides, it calmed me to run my fingers through Mason's ginger and white fur.

"I guess we can both go explore the fair a bit. It's not like Ben will be here any time soon. It sounds like neither Ben nor Night Shadow have any idea when they'll be allowed to leave."

I sighed wondering where I wanted to go. I hadn't had any luck wandering around the fair lately. The first day, I tried wandering and run into people trying to get on my good side so I'd be nicer to them in the competition. Then I'd found a body. I wasn't sure I wanted a repeat of that.

"I'm going to check out the vendors," Deena said. "I heard that someone is selling those interactive feeding toys that you see for cats, but these have a spell on them to make them look like mice."

"I think I saw something about that when I was there," I said. I remembered now. In fact, before Lyn had run me off with her sudden interest in my life, I'd been planning to check out the booth.

"Let's head over there," Deena said. "I'll close the door. I won't lock it. Mason and Bistro should be fine while we're gone."

I nodded. Mason stood up and moved around in his cage.

He glared at me as I walked out, probably aware of what was going on.

Bistro seemed much more laid back about being left behind.

"Bistro is used to it," Deena said, probably noticing my look. "Most of the time, I have free time in the afternoon and go wandering. It's a bit topsy-turvy with Ben being held up, but it's generally the same. He'll keep Mason calm."

"I think Mason will be fine. He's not high strung," I said. "I think he's just annoyed at the change in the routine he was expecting." At least I hoped he'd be fine. Every now and then something happened that he disliked and he'd stay in a grumpy mood for days, taking his displeasure out on me. If I needed magic, he'd be there. That was his role and he honored that, but he'd avoid me except at mealtimes and he wouldn't talk to me unless required.

Deena nodded and we walked out of the building talking. She kept up a flow of conversation. I heard whispers as we left, other judges talking in their rooms.

"Oh my god!" Someone yelled in a room. "I just heard that Shannon Coombs was murdered at the hotel!"

Deena and I exchanged a glance. It was tempting to stay and listen in on the gossip. I noted that Deena was tempted as well. Natalie might be tied up, but it was clear I had someone else who shared my interest in finding out who the murderer was.

Deena paused by the outside door, looking back. I did as well.

A young woman, barely out of high school stepped out of one of the judge's rooms. I couldn't believe that she was a judge.

"Lily!" another voice snapped. "Get back in here!"

The girl slipped inside.

"Not Shannon! I wonder how Olivia is? Should we call her?" This voice sounded like the woman who had wanted Olivia disqualified from the competition. I hoped that Olivia had already heard the news, because I couldn't imagine how awful it would be to hear from someone who clearly disliked you.

"Leave it," a man's voice said. "The police are probably there and if they aren't, she might not know yet."

"But..."

"I said leave it." No arguments.

A police officer hurried down the hallway. I recognized her, but didn't have a name. While I know a lot of people in Waverton, I don't know them all. It pleased me in an odd sort of way to be reminded that I didn't know every police officer in town.

I pulled out my phone and texted Trinity. I didn't get an immediate response as I did with Natalie. Trinity is normal. Natalie is something else.

No more conversations were going on. Deena shrugged and we left through the doors closest to the vendor and craft buildings. Instead of hurrying across the shortest distance, we picked our way through hard earth that held a few ruts of mud from the rain the day before and went around to the main lane that separated the two sides of the fair.

While there were still families around the hay bales, there were fewer that morning taking pictures. I had a feeling that there would be more once the day got started.

Deena hurried by the craft and food building and then past the quilt building. I noted there were plenty of people inside looking around. I tried to remember if there were always that many people looking at crafts or if some of these people were there to try and see where Luanne had died. Then I wondered how many of them had heard that another woman had died as well.

Finally, the vendor building came into view. People streamed in and out, larger crowds than the last few days, but it was Friday. Lots of folks in Waverton, as well as witches from communities in the surrounding area, took Friday off to come to the fair. Tomorrow would be even more crowded.

I breathed in the scent of popcorn and candied apples, both coming from candles at a booth near the door. My stomach was disappointed at the lack of food, but my nose remained pleased. I had no need for scented candles no matter what they did. One was supposed to satisfy cravings, but I noticed no lessening of cravings for a candied apple. My feet shifted a little on the sawdust beneath them. I hoped it was cleaning off my shoes.

Four aisles opened before us with vendors on either side.

Deena paused not certain where to go.

"I think the booth you wanted is towards the back. I passed it just before the specialty library and I think it was the aisle before theirs," I said. I pointed to the left middle aisle which was the one I thought I had walked down.

"You're a gem," Deena said. "I'd have started on the right and worked my way over and spent all my money before I even got there. It's why I haven't purchased one before!"

We started down.

Deena wasn't kidding about her shopping habits. She paused at each booth and talked to every vendor. I learned a lot about the products as I listened and fingered various items and samples. The fudge vendor I'd used for my lunch had samples out. Fortunately, it was a peanut butter fudge and not the same old milk chocolate and pecans I'd purchased the day before.

Deena also took a piece and nodded at the woman.

A large bald man stood behind a stack of books, all of them about a familiar superhero. He smiled when he saw Deena.

"Deena!"

"Jack!" Deena said, throwing her arms open wide. They hugged. Jack even gave her a kiss on the cheek.

I noted he wore very tight jeans and a t-shirt with a dragon on it. His eyes were brilliant green and he smiled every bit as easily as Deena, though there was something less genuine in his than in hers.

"I heard you were here," he said.

"Always. I love Waverton."

"This time might be trying," he said.

"It's so hard to believe. Luanne would have been in my class, you know." Deena had to crane her neck to look up at him. I leafed lightly through his books. They looked vaguely interesting, but I'm not one for superheroes.

"Of course. I forgot for a moment that you know everyone." The man smiled, a bit ingratiatingly, I thought. For a moment I wondered if he had entered the working feline class, but then I realized he was the author. It could easily be just how he interacted with people.

"I do, don't I?" Deena gave a small chuckle before moving on.

"I heard that someone else died," the author said as she turned.

"It's why we're out here and not practicing," Deena said.

"You don't need practice."

"This is Jade Owlens. It's her first time judging."

The bald man nodded at me. "A pleasure, I'm sure." He held out a hand.

I shook it, not sure if he meant it was his pleasure or mine to meet him. The way he acted, it could have gone either way. He did not give me a name. I suppose he thought that I would just recognize him.

I was saved from saying anything when a mixed group of teenagers came up and started asking questions. A brief flicker of annoyance crossed the author's face and then he was back to his usual smile and pleasantries, as if he'd never been interrupted.

"Don't mind Jack," Deena said. "His ego is bigger than Bistro's tummy."

I laughed along with Deena.

Glancing back, I noticed that Jack was watching us walk away, frowning. It almost seemed as if he had something to say. I wondered if he knew something.

"Did he know Luanne?" I asked.

"They dated for a time," Deena said. "So far as I know they broke up amicably."

I wanted to press for more details. In books, a disgruntled ex was always who the police looked at first. I wanted to find Tom or maybe Lina at the WBI and let them know about him. Of course, the WBI ought to already know about him if he was an ex. They were very quick about background checks.

Deena continued her meandering, talking to a vendor here or there. I glanced back more than once and each time it seemed like Jack was staring at us. His expression made me shiver.

Finally, we reached the food game station. The cost of the game, a maze of food spelled to look like mice that ran around, was higher than I could afford for something Mason would probably enjoy for a day or so, if at all. He wasn't a huge eater, though like all cats he was very aware of his stomach.

Deena, however, didn't bat an eye as she purchased one. "Bistro will love this," she told me after she chit-chatted with the vendor. It seemed like she had something personal to say to all of them and she easily introduced herself to everyone.

"You're good at this," I said. "I ought to hire you to go out and talk about my café," I said. I mean, I wasn't shy, but I also didn't go talk to everyone.

"Do you need to build up your business?" Deena asked, looking at me, concern in her eyes.

"I'm actually okay," I said. "I think if I had someone like you around, I'd be better than okay and have to hire more staff!"

Deena put a hand on my arm. "See, you're from a small town where you know people. You naturally talk to those people you know. I'm from a larger town and I have to go meet everyone. And, I've found, that as a judge, it helped me to know who I was working with. Every competition is different and the expectations are different. Waverton's fair is small compared to some, but it's a good springboard for competitors to test out what they're doing and a way to get points if they and their familiar are close to finishing out a grand championship, which isn't as easy to do in the witch world as it is in the dog or cat world."

"Are you saying I need to be out introducing myself?" I asked.

"It wouldn't hurt," Deena said. "And consider having some of your employees work a vendor booth next year. Even if you have to hire someone just for that. It'll get your name out among witches who aren't local. They're more likely to visit your coffee shop if they know you and spend time with your familiars if they know the name. More people will come to the events you judge if they know you and respect you. Don't ever forget that one of the big reasons judges move up in the competition world is because of the draw they have."

I appreciated the thoughts on the booth. I'd been considering getting one this year. Mom would have helped out and I could have worked longer hours. Most of my employees were part-time, so it would have been easy to increase hours. Then, LaDona had come around and offered me the judgeship. It had all seemed too much.

Besides, the familiars were a big part of my café and it seemed like a good idea to have them in the booth. Deciding who should be there was a big decision. I mean, of course, Mason would be there even though he's not available for adoption, but I needed to figure out who else.

"Do you do booths at any of the competitions?" I asked.

Deena shook her head. "I'm not running a shop."

From what I could tell, neither were a lot of these people. The main rescue had a booth, but Peggy's parrot rescue didn't, nor did the equine familiar rescue people. They didn't actually take in horses but rather placed them with locals who had space and could take them in if the families couldn't care for the familiar after a witch died.

The café was both a coffee shop and a bit of a rescue. There was a coffee vendor in the food dome from out of town. Would people be open to another one handing out samples or coupons in the vendor building? And would I need a license for that? Those were questions that I been debating when LaDona had approached me and the idea of a booth had fallen by the wayside.

I followed Deena as she talked to the vendors down the next aisle. I saw Trinity and chatted with her for a few. Deena came up and made small talk.

"I sometimes envy people who work in libraries," Deena said. "So many good books to explore and possibly read. Tell me, what made you decide on a library position?"

"I liked the fact that there were set hours. And I'd always be learning. The hours and pay let me hike on my days off and enjoy the outside," Trinity said. "It's not quite enough to afford my own horse, at least not yet, but I'm hopeful that in a few years I can swing it."

I knew Trinity loved riding and hiking. I had no idea she was in the market for a horse.

"Will you be looking for a horse familiar or just a horse?" Deena asked.

"I was going to check out familiars, but if I can't afford one or if none fall in love with me, I'd go with an ordinary. It's really riding that I love. And I've been without a familiar for a few years now. I don't do a ton of spells. The library doesn't allow spells while working, of course, but even at home, I don't think of spells, per se, so I don't miss having the backup."

Trinity had a few natural talents, like sometimes being able to read minds, but she was right. She didn't often do spells. Natalie was much more likely to do something like that.

"You are certainly in the right area to be shopping around," Deena said. We wandered off, while I gave Trinity a quick wave.

The morning passed meeting other vendors. As we were about to leave the building, I turned and noticed Deena's author friend, Jack standing at a booth not far behind us, staring at us. Or maybe he was staring at me. I couldn't be certain.

19

Deena left without noticing Jack. I didn't know if I should say anything. I mean, maybe he was just taking a quick break to stretch his legs. Maybe he thought he recognized me, but wasn't sure from where. I kept telling myself stuff like that.

Deena got a text from Ben. He was on his way.

"Finally," she said. "I know the police have to do their jobs, but it seems like if someone is expected to be somewhere they could hurry up and interview them."

It did seem like that, but I had a feeling that being on time for a competition judge rehearsal was not as important to them as it was to us.

"Go get something to eat, honey. I know you didn't eat lunch yesterday and we don't need a repeat of that," Deena said. "I'm going to go back to the room. I know I won't miss lunch even if it's a bit late."

I wasn't very hungry. I was still upset about Julia. I walked towards the food dome, taking a moment to call Tom. I got nothing. I texted Tyson, asking if the new murder in town allowed Julia to go free. After all, Waverton wasn't a large town with a ton of murders. Chances were the two women had been murdered by the same person.

By the time Tyson texted me back, I had gotten a cinnamon roll, not exactly a healthy lunch, but nothing else sounded good. So far the police weren't letting Julia go although Tyson admitted that the second murder made it likely they would do so soon.

I hoped the second murder had opened up their investigations.

I settled at an outdoor table to eat my snack. The day was cool, but there were plenty of other people around. Some had lunch items, others were still snacking, like me.

The flavor of the cinnamon burst out of the roll though I found the frosting a little too sweet for my palate that morning. Normally, I loved it, but clearly, I was still upset by Julia's arrest.

"I can't believe there was another murder." It was the women I'd seen talking in the quilt aisle after Luanne died.

"They arrested someone, too," another voice said, "but they must have the wrong person."

"Or maybe she set it up to look like that," the first woman suggested.

"I wouldn't put it past her. Anyone who would kill another witch just because they criticized her quilting—and to be honest, the evenness of those stitches does make it look machine done—would do anything, including having someone else kill another person."

I didn't recognize the last voice. I risked looking around.

Definitely the same women. The older woman had sharp eyes and she noticed me looking.

She lowered her voice.

I turned back to my cinnamon roll, but found I had less appetite. These women weren't saying anything that others wouldn't say about Julia. I worried this incident would follow her. Trinity still got strange looks sometimes, although she'd been cleared of Eric's murder. The Waverton paper had even had a story about how she'd been brave enough to remain in jail while the police worked to draw the murderer out. Some people still thought she might have done it.

Trinity had a job at a library where appearances were far less important. Julia worked retail. Even if she won the competition, I wasn't at all certain her boss would want her extra quilts and projects being sold through the store. Too many people might get offended by having them on sale.

I picked at the pieces of my cinnamon roll here and there. I glanced up as someone sat across from me, breaking into a smile when I saw it was Tyson.

"You aren't working?" I asked.

"I'm working," he said. I noted the button-down shirt and nice slacks. "I got your text when I was on my way to interview the craft section coordinator. I went by the competition building, but a very large woman named Deena said she'd sent you to the food court. I see you're making less than great use of your time."

"Pick up a fork. I'm just not very hungry what with everything going on," I said. "And I worry about what will happen even when the police find the real murderer."

Tyson nodded. He didn't add anything or try to reassure me. I could have used that, but it wasn't his way. He was very honest. He did, however, pick up a fork and start nibbling at my cinnamon roll.

"Are you eating?" he asked. "I know you're upset about Julia, and I haven't been able to be there for you."

"Deena seems intent upon making sure I don't starve," I said.

Tyson frowned, but said nothing.

"She sent me here because the other judge I'm working

with, Ben, is late because he's staying at Natalie's." I made a face. "I guess the police questioned him."

"The WBI stepped in and right now they're questioning everyone. Tom has been taken off suspension because the WBI has taken over. They really just didn't want him pretending to be working the case. Now that none of the officers are working it, Tom will go back to work next week, though he'll be on patrol downtown."

Which meant he was down by the cafe. It would keep him away from the fairgrounds and away from the hotel. I suppose it didn't matter if the WBI closed the case by that time or not. Tom wouldn't be around the crime scenes. I felt bad that my thoughts on who had done it might have gotten him in trouble.

"It's a good thing he had an alibi, too," Tyson said as if sensing my guilt and wanting to make a point. "Otherwise the WBI would have been looking at him as a possible suspect. He was pretty angry with Olivia and Shannon."

"Where was he?" I asked.

"He spent the night in the detox cell after getting drunk and trying to break into the jail to see Julia," Tyson said. "The timing for Shannon's murder doesn't work. The police are fairly certain it happened in the early hours of the morning."

"I hate that he got locked up. I'm surprised they let him work at all."

"I think they thought that was more of a punishment than sending him home. Besides, this way, he's monitored," Tyson went on. "This is why you don't go around asking questions."

"Like I said, a lot of this I got just by listening in on things. Deena asks questions too, you know. Of course, I think she knows half the people at the fair, and is planning to meet the other half."

Tyson gave me a half-smile and looked down at the cinnamon roll. "I can't stop everyone, but I can warn you about the problems. And you could tell Deena to stop playing sleuth, too. Someone could get hurt and not just by being put on suspension. I mean injured or killed."

Tyson didn't have to remind me. We had both almost died last summer. Not because I was playing at being a sleuth. I had gone to check on something at his office and the door was open. I called him and waited outside. He walked in and I followed. I didn't think it was my fault we were almost killed.

Still, it had been a near thing and maybe it ought to make me feel protected that he didn't want me taking any chances. Instead, I felt like a child with an overprotective parent.

I pursed my lips, but said nothing else.

Tyson started to say something more.

I held up a hand. "Just stop, okay? This is my sister and I get to have opinions about what's going on. I can't control what other people do with my opinions. I get to worry and wonder and theorize what might have happened to put her in prison, okay? I'm not going to go around policing my every thought because you're worried that somehow I might do or say something to the wrong person about what I think is going on."

Tyson drew back. His face turned a sort of blotchy reddish color that faded quickly. He swallowed, though he'd not taken a bite.

"I'm not saying you can't have opinions, but you have to be careful who you tell and how you coach them. You don't want the WBI looking at you thinking you're trying to help Julia."

"I'm not," I said.

"Do you have an alibi?" Tyson asked.

"I was home with Mason. They can get a familiar communicator in to talk to him. Familiars don't lie."

Unless of course they'd been spelled. Given the magical

nature of a familiar and the close bond between familiar and witch, it could be difficult to ascertain if a familiar had been spelled. If one had been, it was obvious, but if one hadn't... well, there was always a question.

Tyson held my gaze, clearly thinking exactly what I was thinking. He didn't like my response one bit.

"Look, I was busy. And I was here on time. Deena can vouch for that. And her familiar would be willing to talk to Mason as well and find things out. You know other familiars are often much more attuned to whether another has been spelled, particularly when they've recently talked."

I was reaching. I knew the part about friendly familiars from school, but I didn't know if there was any legal precedent for using that bond in court.

Tyson sighed and looked down. "Just be careful, okay? I care about you and I'm doing what I can to take care of you. And your sister."

"I know," I agreed. "But I'm not a child and I don't like being treated like one."

He nodded and pushed the plate which still held a third of the cinnamon roll back towards me. I had even less appetite when he left.

I noticed the women who had been talking looking over at me as he walked away. Then the whispers started. I wondered if they thought I'd done exactly what Tyson had said would be believable. Then I worried they might go to the WBI with that information.

Suddenly I wished I'd never been hired as a judge. I wouldn't have the stress of a new job along with the worry about my sister. I would know who I could and couldn't trust in the café. And most of all, I wouldn't have had the access to go questioning someone in the horse barn.

Tyson was right. If Shannon had been killed by negative magic the way Luanne was, if the magical signature was at all similar to mine, I could be in the crosshairs. On the one hand, I really wanted to know how she died, but maybe not knowing would be a good thing.

I picked up my plate and turned to back to the competition building. I ran into Lina, the WBI witch near the trash. With her crossed arms and a long suffering look, I knew she'd been standing there waiting for me. She might even have heard my conversation with Tyson.

20

Lina's red hair was braided around the top of her head almost like a cartoon Swiss maiden. Her eyes were pale and always looked as if she weren't quite looking at you but through you. She was standing on one foot, the other toe down. Her legs were crossed just as her arms. She stood a few feet from the trash, not a finger moving.

Her face was set. I'd say she wasn't pleased, but I wasn't sure I'd ever seen Lina look pleased.

"Jade. I think we need to talk. Again." She didn't wait for me to acknowledge the order, just turned around, expecting me to follow her.

"I think Deena is waiting for me in the competition office," I said, pausing to put my stuff in the trash.

Lina didn't bother to answer. I sighed, wondering if I should turn around and head the other way. I couldn't quite make myself do it, but as I considered it, I felt the slightest pulse of compulsion. She'd spelled me. No wonder she was so confident.

A non-WBI witch, even a police officer in a town like

Waverton, would be in a lot of trouble for a compulsion spell. But WBI witches got away with a lot. Of course, they were vetted and re-vetted over and over again. Since this past summer, I'd looked into their training and what it took to be part of the WBI.

I let my feet lead me through the fair to a small tent near the entrance. I walked inside, only to find I was in an office building. A window to the outside overlooked Louisville. A small teleport, then.

Teleport booths, as we called them, took a lot of magic to set up and maintain. At least six witches, normally, unless one had a particular talent, but even then you needed another witch to anchor at the other end. The WBI didn't mess around with fairs, apparently. Here I thought I had wanted to know more about the WBI, but the more I learned, the less I wanted to know.

I glanced back and it appeared that I'd walked out of the broom closet. The window was to my right and a hallway filled with closed doors loomed in the other direction, which was where Lina was walking. I noted the carpeting was smooth and pale, with no streaks of blood. The walls were a uniform beige with white corkboard ceiling panels overhead and florescent lights that buzzed like a fleet of mosquitos on a quest for blood.

My shoes were silent on the carpet. Despite the stains of mud on them, nothing broke off to leave tracks, though I almost wished it did. I hadn't asked to go there. And I hadn't even been able to tell anyone where I was. I suspected that if I tried to text Deena, my phone wouldn't work.

Lina waited by the third door on the left. When I reached her, she opened it and I went inside. I breathed out a small sigh that wasn't quite relief. The desk across the way was covered in paper, held an old black rotary phone, and a black mesh inbox. Bookshelves in a mahogany-colored wood rose behind it. In front of the desk were two chairs with blue upholstery. A single picture of the bridge between Louisville and Indiana hung on the plain wall.

"Have a seat," Lina said, pointing to the chairs. She seated herself behind the desk. I thought I noticed the faintest hint of dust. Perhaps the office wasn't used much, which would explain the old phone and lack of a computer.

I sat. The chairs were more comfortable than I had expected, the upholstery surprisingly thick. The room smelled of old books and dust, reminding me of the specialty library. The office definitely didn't get used much. I wondered if this was Lina's. It certainly wasn't an interrogation room.

"You heard about the murder this morning." Lina looked up at me, waiting for a response. It wasn't a question.

"Our third judge, Ben, was staying at the hotel and Deena's familiar talked to his familiar about the fact that he would be late."

Lina nodded. She didn't make a note. She'd have a recording spell. Always. I wondered why there was so much paper. I wanted to ask. Knew better than to do so.

"Where were you last night?" Lina pulled a pen out of a drawer and looked around for a paper. She pulled something out of an inbox, glanced at it, and then turned it over, prepared to take notes. As if she read my mind and knew I felt odd that she wasn't taking notes.

"I was at home," I said. "Sleeping. Tyson doesn't sleep over, so it was just me and my familiar, Mason. You can get a familiar communicator to ask him."

"We probably will," Lina said, writing down what I said.

I waited, offering nothing. At least I listened to Tyson about that. It was only when I talked to people like Tom that I blurted things out.

"Did you know Shannon?" Lina asked.

"No." I itched to explain that I knew of her, but better to say nothing than to offer something they could use.

"Really?" Lina raised an eyebrow.

"I'd never talked to her to my knowledge. I can't say that I knew her," I repeated, attempting to clarify with giving nothing away.

"You know her family though, right?" Lina already knew the answer to that.

"Natalie and I talked to Olivia in the fair barn," I said. "I later learned that Olivia had a cousin who quilted. Unless there was a strong family resemblance, I wouldn't have recognized Shannon."

"Shannon had a magical signature that was similar to your sister's," Lina said, waiting.

I held her gaze. I might have guessed that given that I suspected Olivia and Shannon, but I hadn't known.

The silence went on. I had read enough mysteries to know this was a technique used to get people to talk. I mentally recited what Tyson said about not offering information.

Finally, Lina looked down at the paper as if she needed it to formulate another question. I had been around her enough to know she needed no such thing.

"I went to the café this morning to pick up your magical signature," Lina said. "Would you like to know what I found?"

I didn't know what she found. I tried both yes and no answers. Both could be used against me.

"I'm sure you'll tell me," I said.

Lina waited. The silence began to itch at me. I wanted to say more. I wanted conversation to fill the discomfort of the silence. I read about sleuths who were questioned saying they were comfortable with silence and didn't feel a need to fill it. I was hanging on to silence by my fingernails, which seemed to be sliding down a chalkboard making me cringe.

Finally, Lina spoke. "Your magical signature is nothing like your sister's. It doesn't match the signature in the hotel room nor does it hold any similarities to the negative magic at the fair."

I bit my lip to keep from asking why I was there.

Lina let the silence stretch.

"That doesn't mean you don't know something," she finally said. Again, that pause, waiting for me to fill it.

Except she was wrong. I wanted to blurt out everything I had done and what had happened and that Tom had been suspended because he listened and how my boyfriend wasn't happy with me for having an opinion and being willing to share it. I wanted to tell her that everyone at the fair was talking and that she'd get more gossip if she talked to Deena because Deena had a way about her that got people to talk.

And then I snarkily considered whether to suggest she take some lessons from Deena because I'd already told her more than I intended to tell Lina, and my reticence wasn't just because Tyson told me to keep my mouth shut.

"I heard, though, that the competition coordinator is concerned that you'll pass a murderer through. Which of your entrants do you think would have killed Luanne? And then Shannon?"

I rolled my eyes and sighed. "I know a few of the people, mostly casually. Others are just names. I went over the list with Deena and Ben yesterday in terms of how they work with their familiar. It's knowledge that will help me look for certain tells as a judge, not to investigate who would murder another entrant. It seems really competitive, but I haven't heard that anyone was killed to win any other years."

Lina gave me a tight smile. "And what do you think about your sister's arrest?'

"That she didn't do it." I practically snapped. Like I'd think anything else.

"I heard she was a pretty straight-arrow as far as positive magic. I've even talked to her boss and it sounds like none of her spells even gets into the gray zone of not quite positive. Julia sounds like she's really a Miss Mary Sunshine, which must get annoying."

I waited for a question. Tyson had said I should always wait for a question before answering. I might have been blurting right and left not long after Luanne was killed, but now I was steadier and reminding myself of his words fifteen times a minute or more.

Tyson was already unhappy with me for having opinions. I could only imagine how he'd react if I said something to the WBI that got Julia in more trouble.

Lina sighed and shook her head. "Your attorney boyfriend has been coaching you well. I don't remember you as being this quiet last time."

I shrugged. "Maybe I knew more last time."

Lina held my gaze, daring me to press that point.

"I think you have ideas and thoughts about this. I noticed you and your blonde friend over talking to Shannon's cousin."

I'd already admitted talking to Olivia in the barn. I made a face, trying to decide how to answer.

"I heard she was considered a favorite in the working equine class. I chatted with her a bit, getting tips on things. I can't actually talk to the cat entrants because I judge them, but I could pick up pointers from someone in another species class."

I hoped Lina hadn't talked to Olivia. I hadn't made a point of asking who would hate Luanne, but I had sort of asked questions about the murder.

Lina made a note on the paper. Or maybe she doodled. I couldn't see it and given that she would be able to magically replay the whole conversation, I didn't know why she was scribbling anything.

"Were you surprised that Shannon was killed?"

I frowned. "I guess?" I said. "I mean I wasn't expecting anyone to be killed. It's not like people are randomly murdered in Waverton on a regular basis."

"But Shannon. It seemed like she and Olivia were the prime contenders for the murders if the police decided it wasn't your sister. Did that bother you?"

"I guess it bothered me that someone else is dead. I didn't know Shannon, so I can't say that I'm personally grieving, but she was a person." I couldn't imagine what Lina was getting at.

"It's strange to me that Julia was arrested on circumstantial evidence and one of the people others were gossiping about turns up dead. It narrows the field. By any standards, it seems that Olivia and Shannon were reasonably close. Not joined at the hip close but close cousins making it hard to imagine her murdering a family member."

I looked first at one wall and then out the window while raising my shoulders in a shrug. I didn't know what Lina wanted.

"I guess I'm looking for an *opinion*." Lina stressed the last word. She had been listening in on my conversation with Tyson.

"About?" I asked, jumping in, annoyed that she'd clearly been listening.

"Who do you think did it? You know the town better than I do." Lina leaned back and waited.

"I don't know," I said. "I mean the entrants are all pushy and act like they want to get in my good graces, but I can't see anyone murdering anyone over this. It seems like people love to criticize the crafters, so I can't see a disgruntled crafter murdering someone over their criticism, either."

"Luanne and Shannon had been in other competitions. Shannon, always with magical crafts. She's very well-known. Has a few books out. Your sister has probably read them. Shannon judged at a bunch of fairs, magical and ordinary. She talked about quilting even to ordinary folks. It was her thing. I think your sister is more of a general fabric art person, is that what you call it?" Lina asked.

"I think that's how Julia describes herself. I know she quilts and she's good, but she says she doesn't love quilting just for the sake of it the way others do. She loves sewing and particularly loves hand sewing. She likes big projects like making the blinds at my café."

Lina nodded. "Not clothing though?"

I shrugged again. "She can make clothing and she enjoys it, but not like she does the big projects. If you needed a dozen quilts for a bed and breakfast, she'd be all over that. It's like getting something really big accomplished is her passion."

Julia had, in fact, embroidered a dozen table cloths for the bed and breakfast on the edge of town and loved every minute of it. She also sewed their holiday placemats, the swags they hung over the windows to keep the garland from shedding on their curtains, and did a small lap quilt to lay at the foot of each bed for the holidays.

Lina nodded. "Exactly. But she enters the competition here every year."

"It raises her profile," I said. "They don't have a category for the kinds of projects she loves so she usually enters the quilting contest. She does very well because her talents run to fabric."

"We've noticed. There's nothing fabric in her home that doesn't hold a bit of a spell," Lina said. "Which was kind of weird that the one thing without it was the item stolen, don't you think?"

"I guess."

"So Shannon wouldn't have been in direct competition with her?" Lina asked.

"In this competition, they were both in quilts. I don't know if there's a size or a type subcategory, but ultimately they would have been up against each other in the broader quilt section, yes."

"And Luanne criticized both of them?"

"I only heard her criticize the quilt by Shannon," I said. "From what I heard around the fair, she could have gone after every quilter."

"I found four quilts that she's said to have praised," Lina said. I waited. She didn't tell me which ones.

"She was very critical of the other entrants as well," Lina added. "Let's see, your local person, Lyn Upton, was too fat to compete easily and anyone that lazy shouldn't even try."

Lina looked up after quoting that.

Lyn was a little curvy but most of her weight was in her breasts. My hips were wider than hers so I hated to think what Luanne thought of me.

"And let's see, Hal Rendell, one of the out of towners, had such a stick up his butt she was surprised he could walk across the stage. Everything he and his familiar did made them look like they were puppets being played by the same poor puppet master."

Again, the pause and wait.

Lina read off a few more insults to people who would be showing in my category. Some of the names were familiar and I felt myself bristling in their defense much like I had for Lyn. Others meant nothing to me, but considering how I felt about the people I did know, I could only imagine those insults were equally unwarranted.

"You hadn't heard any of that?" Lina asked.

"I knew people didn't like her, but other than the one

time in the craft building where she criticized Shannon's quilt in front of me, I hadn't heard her say anything, really." I was still trying to figure out what Lina wanted from me.

"Luanne had a particular hatred for Ben, did you know that?"

I shook my head.

"As did Shannon."

Lina let that hang. I suddenly understood why Ben had had to wait to be questioned. My stomach twisted. I liked Ben. I didn't want him to be a murderer. I remembered what Deena had said about being good at reading people. She liked Ben. I couldn't imagine her liking Ben if he were a murderer.

"Nothing to say?" Lina asked.

My mouth was dry and I had to try and wet my lips a few times. "I like Ben. I only just met him, but he was nice to me. He seems like a really good guy."

"At least you have an opinion about someone," Lina said. "The negative magic the murderer used has a signature that's not dissimilar to his. It's about as exact a match as you can get to the spell used on the scarf which strangled Luanne but only slightly similar to Ben's. We can't rule him out, though, especially because he had ease of access. His room was one floor up from hers and above the room next door."

Which was close enough for a magical attack if needed. It would take some power, which I had a feeling Ben had or Lina wouldn't be mentioning it.

"Does this mean Julia is going to be released?" I asked.

Lina narrowed her eyes at me.

"I mean, you can't believe there are two unrelated murders in town, can you? My sister couldn't have murdered Shannon." I could almost hear Tyson yelling at me, but this was my sister. It would probably look equally odd if I didn't ask.

"As I said, it seems as if these are related. That doesn't

mean the police are going to let Julia go. The evidence, although circumstantial, is strong. Her not being able to murder Shannon suggests an accomplice. Your magical signature pretty much removes you from the equation. However, she has a boyfriend, devoted enough to get himself suspended from the investigation. And, like you, she has plenty of friends in town."

Lina leaned back.

I glared.

"I still don't know what you want from me," I said.

Lina smiled. "You can go for now. We have it."

She didn't move. After a moment, I stood up and went to the door. My hand shook as I opened it, eager to get out of there and worried about what she had gotten from me that she needed.

Once I got back to the fair through the teleport room in the old broom closet, I quickly made my way to the competition building. Ben was already there, talking to Deena.

"I thought we'd lost you," Deena said brightly.

"I got questioned by the WBI," I said, hanging my head. I probably looked as miserable as I felt.

The room smelled like garlic and I noticed a bit of pasta on a plate. I wondered if Ben had brought leftovers or if Deena had. I wished I had something savory to share instead of the too-sweet cinnamon roll which hadn't done anything for me when I ate it and was now threatening to return.

Deena, of course, made the expected shocked exclamations. Ben remained silent, shaking his head.

"They think I did it, don't they?" he asked after Deena had given me a hug.

"You're definitely a suspect. Proximity and the fact that you apparently have had run-ins with Shannon in prior competitions," I said, pulling away from Deena.

Mason was sitting in his kennel staring at me. I knew he

wanted to know what was going on. It was one thing for me to bring him there with me, but I'd left him alone for half a day. And I hadn't explained what I was up to. He'd know some from when I spoke. Cats say they don't understand, but they mostly do. It's almost a game to them to pretend they don't know something.

"No!" Deena said again, shaking her head. "Tell me everything."

So I told her what Lina had asked me, as much as I could remember. Oddly, I found it hard to know exactly what had happened in the room. I did remember the discomfort of sitting there and looking at her, but the exact words were fading from my mind. Probably another spell. The WBI had everything and they used it too, which frustrated me. At least last time I hadn't known anything they needed to wipe.

After I explained why I was late, Ben took over for his tale. Mason still sat close to the edge of the kennel, but I moved over to put a hand on his head.

He didn't have any snarky comments, but he pushed against it and washed a paw.

"I was questioned by the WBI as well. I was asked to wait by the Waverton police, but soon enough the WBI took over. Most of the people trying to leave were segregated by floor and were asked not to talk. They had a witch there watching. I guess one group kept whispering and they put a silence spell on them."

My eyes widened. Teachers would do that sometimes in school, but I'd never heard of such a thing used on adults. When used improperly, it could be considered negative magic, and as such, any use was considered gray. Teachers could get away with it and parents, but if someone used it too often, they could get a warning.

Deena clicked her tongue at the comment.

Ben rested his forehead on his hand. "It's hard to

remember what they asked me. I know they talked about my encounter with Shannon and why we disliked each other. It wasn't just that she thought I wasn't higher-level judge material, we dated for a bit, but the long-distance thing didn't work. And there's a certain level of artistic jealousy when one is doing better than the other. I'm ashamed to say that I was the one not doing quite as well."

Deena went over and gave Ben a hug. He returned it with his arms but he didn't stand to fall into her embrace, leaving her leaning awkwardly over him.

When Deena backed off, Ben talked a little more. He remembered being asked about the way the breakup went. He knew Shannon had broken it off, but he couldn't remember what he had said about it.

"Memory wipe," Deena said.

"It's hard for me to remember what went on too," I added, rubbing Mason's ears.

I can probably search your memory for artifacts, Mason assured me. *I can help you get those back. Night Shadow can do that for Ben if he's worried.*

I told Deena and Ben what Mason had said.

"I've heard of that," Deena said. "Never needed it because I tend to remember things pretty well, but my aunt had dementia and her familiar was able to help her quite a bit until she was well into late stage."

I tried to decide which impressed me more. The fact that familiars could do that or the fact that someone had been creative enough to come up with that idea to help with dementia. Of course, witches with dementia could have personality changes and get very negative in their magic. I'd encountered one such witch just last summer. Sometimes, though, it was ordinary dementia and just made them forgetful.

Ben nodded and rubbed Night Shadow's head. He was silent for a bit.

"I think we'll need a quieter place. We do need to go over the roles again. We ought to do that," Ben said finally.

So we all turned our chairs around and talked about what each of us would be doing during the competition. Deena would be examining the felines. Ben would be the judge that tempted the familiars with toys and then would make sure each person got their familiar and took them over to Deena. I would be watching to be sure that there wasn't any magic going on and that everyone who wasn't being examined was staying in their places. Ben would help with that, but it wouldn't be his main focus.

During the next part, I'd be handing out paper and pencils for people. Ben and Deena would do the timing. We'd all be looking to see who finished first.

I appreciated that all my jobs were pretty easy. If I got stage fright or something, someone would be covering for me.

We ran through the competition, having each of us play the role we'd have as a judge. Deena refereed making suggestions about what might be going on. Finally, it was over.

"And now we can stretch our legs and go for a late lunch," Deena said. "Then we can go over any questions that come up while we're out and before we all take off. How about we meet back here in about an hour?"

I agreed. I still wasn't hungry, the cinnamon roll sitting heavy in my stomach. I rubbed Mason's ears. He wasn't pleased that I was leaving again and he flattened them. Still, I didn't much have a choice. He had to participate in monitoring the feline entrants. His job, too, was the easiest of all three of the familiars.

I stood up and headed out of the building. I still hadn't had a chance to look at everything around the fair. I wanted to wander through the food and photography room and the goat barn and I did kind of want to finish the craft building, although my stomach knotted just thinking about it. Now that ribbons were up, I wondered if Julia had won anything for her quilt or if she'd been disqualified because of her arrest.

The day was cool but pleasantly sunny. A slight breeze hit me and brought in the ripe smells of horses and goats and other small creatures. I decided I'd head towards the barns. Groups of adults as well as families with kids walked along the main path between the vendor buildings and the barn.

I heard kids eagerly ask for their fair favorites, hot dogs or cotton candy. The cotton candy vendor stayed along the midway with the rides. I hadn't even considered going in there, though it had once been one of my favorite places.

Maybe tomorrow evening Tyson would go with me and we could hit some of the rides. I loved the octopus. If he was still too busy with Julia's case, perhaps Natalie would be off. She normally worked days and let someone else take over the evening shift.

I heard a snort from one of the horses and the stamping of hooves. Some voices talking. A child had clearly asked about riding and lessons and the owner of the horse was talking to them about how learning to care for the horse was just as important as riding. Given the pitch of the child's voice, I wasn't sure they were old enough to really understand, but it was never too early to start impressing such things upon them.

I got to the goat building and wandered in. Goats aren't super popular as familiars so there were plenty of non-familiar goats in there, too. A woman sat at the entry spinning thread from goat wool. A display of the wool from the moment it was sheered to a small piece of fabric that had been handwoven showed the process.

It's the sort of thing Julia could have added a ton of historic details to. She'd have wanted to know the spell the woman was doing when she wove the thread. I felt a low tingle on my arms from magic and supposed it had to come from her.

Children stood to the far side where two small goats stood in a pen. One let the child pet its head. The other was watching the spinning wheel like a cat about to pounce. It was a pleasant scene and I wanted to stay there for a bit to put the stress of the murders behind me and just enjoy the fair.

The spinner smiled at me and I smiled back. The tingle lessened along my arms. The moment she went back to concentrating on her thread the tingle showed up again. Definitely her spell.

I walked down the aisle looking at the various goats. There were stalls of cute little black and white pygmy goats, along with the larger brown Nubian goats, which I read were good for milk. On the other side were the goats that were good for shearing, like the Angoras and Cashmeres. I glanced back at the woman near the front and wondered what sort of goats she had.

I had nearly reached the end of the long aisle when the group of women I kept running into came around from the other direction.

"Celia!" the older woman exclaimed, though about what I didn't know. She turned to look at her companion, frowning. The name rang a bell.

"I'm just saying I think Olivia could have been involved, and as you heard, so did Barb," the woman who had be Celia said. It hit me then that Natalie had talked about her and so had Deena. Celia had a canine familiar.

"Barb doesn't know shit," the older woman snapped.

Another woman tried to shush her, probably worried that the sounds might carry through the barn to the unknown Barb.

I paused to look more closely at a particularly lovely Cashmere goat alone in its pen. My eyes didn't quite focus on the information tag while I listened but I hoped I looked sufficiently interested.

"Look, Barb knew Shannon and she knows Olivia slightly. Olivia is quite keen on Traci and chances are with that local poser woman and Shannon out of the way, Traci's quilt will place first," Celia said.

The older woman glared at Celia. "I think you're jumping to conclusions. If Olivia is behind this, then the local woman didn't murder anyone, and she should be freed and her quilt would then be eligible to place again."

Celia shrugged. "It's neither here nor there. I mean, chances are Kandy Karmen and I will place and then go onto all working familiars. I can beat Olivia even if the police aren't smart enough to arrest her. It's just too bad that Traci is likely to place thanks to her meddling."

The woman passed me, hardly noticing the Cashmere goat, which I thought was a shame. It was gorgeous. Unfortunately, I couldn't just turn around and follow them.

I wandered slowly, straining to hear more but a different goat bleated loudly enough to keep me from hearing anything more. Soon enough I was around the corner. There were more people there with their goats and some were answering questions. I paused here and there, but none of them ever struck up a conversation with me, which was too bad.

I could have talked more to them and asked, searching for the mysterious Barb, but I was tired, mentally, at least. The physical fatigue was probably from not having enough to eat during the day.

I considered grabbing something else from the food dome, but most things were heavy and greasy and my stomach wasn't up for that. Maybe I'd head out to the deli when I got home and get a sandwich. I always liked Irene's Deli and I could get a something made exactly the way I wanted.

For once my stomach didn't knot at the thought of food. Good. That was a plan. Hopefully, it wouldn't take too long to get questions answered about the competition tomorrow.

I walked slowly towards the competition building, looking at my phone, noting that I still had a good twenty minutes before I needed to be back. A short detour through the food and photography building should take up that time.

Just then I got a text from Natalie.

The WBI had finished up at the hotel. Her dad was leaving and she was back in charge.

I heard they're looking at one of the feline competition judges, I sent.

At first, they were. The text came back about the time my finger was lifting off the send. I shook my head at Natalie's ability to anticipate a text.

My phone rang. Natalie. She had time to talk now. I found a place to stand that wasn't in the way of the people wandering around nearly as aimlessly as I was and answered.

"What happened?" I asked.

"At first they were all over Ben, the judge," Natalie said. "He wasn't happy to be waiting for so long. He had his cat in a carrier and everything and they didn't seem worried about water."

That annoyed me. You'd think the WBI would be better about things like that.

"Anyway, they talked to him and they still seemed interested, but didn't have a way to connect him to the murder. I guess his magical signature didn't have many similarities. Now they're back off to consider the cousin, Olivia," Natalie said quietly.

"Wow." I didn't know what to say. I was clearly not a very good judge of character. I'd liked Olivia.

"I know you didn't think she could have done it, but the WBI are interested," Natalie said.

"I heard that with Shannon and Julia out of the competition her friend Traci might take first place for quilts, or something." Maybe it was just place at all. I should have gone into the craft building and figured out which of the quilts belonged to Traci. I could see if she'd won anything.

"I heard Traci isn't just a friend," Natalie corrected. "And that they've been having problems. Gossip is that perhaps Olivia was doing this to get into Traci's good graces again. Unfortunately, Traci isn't at the hotel."

I smiled at Natalie's use of the word 'unfortunately.' I had a feeling Traci might find it very fortunate, as Nat was likely to have done her own interrogation, which would have been warm and friendly and far more likely to solicit information than the WBI.

"I'm glad Ben isn't a suspect any longer," I said.

"I'm not sure he's completely off the radar," Natalie said. "He and Shannon used to date and I guess the breakup wasn't exactly pretty. Of course, they got that information from Olivia and now that they're looking at her again, they might be rethinking that. If it's true, then they might start looking at Ben again, especially if Olivia has an alibi."

"How do you find this stuff out?" I asked.

"I listen," Natalie said. "People talk in hotel reception areas. No one thinks anyone is really listening. Between that and being willing to ask questions, I can find out just about anything."

"Ben did mention that he and Shannon had broken up. He said it had to do with two artists in a relationship. I guess he had some professional jealousy of her success," I said.

"So it could be him."

"I can't imagine it. I mean, I know I don't think Olivia did it either, but it's way easier to see her committing murder than it is Ben. I've been working with him. He's a nice guy."

Lyn Upton walked by and gave me an overly friendly smile and wave. I waved back. She started to come over and then noticed the phone and slipped into the building.

"I ought to go and get back to the competition building," I said. I started walking over there. I still had a few minutes but Mason would appreciate the company. Lyn was far less likely to go wandering in and start talking to me if I was in the judge's room. At least I hoped that was true.

2 2

There weren't many judging issues to go over, and Ben was every bit as fidgety as I was. Deena suggested we all take off and maybe come in a little early for the competition the next day. I packed up Mason and his things without complaint. Ben was equally quiet. Even Deena didn't keep a running dialogue.

The second murder had gotten to everyone.

"I'll let you know what Bistro thinks of his feeding toy," Deena said.

I nodded and smiled. While it might be great, I didn't see how I could afford such a thing for Mason. He glared at me as if he knew what I was thinking. We'd talk at home.

The exit for the judges to our parking lot was behind the competition building and I was grateful for that now that the fair was busier. Even the short walk to my car had plenty of kids talking and pointing at the cats. Given the crowds and the general make-up of fairgoers in prior years, I figured plenty of them were ordinary kids who had no idea how special our cats were.

Even the witch children probably got a kick out of seeing

feline familiars. Canine familiars might go everywhere, but cats didn't often do so.

I smiled at the kids, but kept Mason's carrier close to the front of my body as I hurried out towards my car. I didn't want to get stopped by anyone. Deena seemed just as eager to escape, and Ben had already left.

When I got out of the parking lot, I was glad to be going away from the main entrance where a line of cars waited to get into the parking lot. It happened every year. About half the farmers took advantage of the line to put out farm-to-consumer late-season vegetables and some of their hand-made food products in small stands along the route. The other half hated the congestion and complained to anyone who would listen.

I'd like to think I was the sort to put out something nice, but had a feeling that year after year, I'd start thinking like the folks complaining.

Going away from the fair was easier than getting to it and I made decent time on the way home. I considered stopping at Irene's but Mason's ears were angled out to the sides, though not flattened. He wasn't a happy cat. I needed to get him home first.

As I had the day before, I left his stuff in the car and lugged the carrier up the steps. Mason reminded me he could have taken the steps himself by shifting his weight in the carrier each time I lifted a foot. A headache started at the base of my neck while I hung onto him and the stair rail equally tightly.

Finally, I made it up the stairs and opened the door. For payback, I didn't let him out of the carrier until we were well inside. We were both out of sorts.

I fed Mason and looked around the apartment. Something about it didn't feel quite right. I sniffed. The air smelled wrong.

I reached down to touch Mason's head while he ate.

"I smell something wrong," I said. In addition to smelling something wrong, things felt wrong. My heart beat too quickly and my hands began to sweat.

Mason looked up from his food and sniffed. He paused and walked towards the center of the main room. I did a small spell to let me telepathically stay in contact with him even though I wasn't touching him.

I smell it too, he said. *A witch did magic in here.*

Still here? I thought at him. If someone were in the apartment, I didn't want to give away any more than I already had.

I don't believe so. The scent isn't that strong. Mason kept his nose in the air, his mouth open just a bit, getting every bit of scent essence to tell him something.

My arms tingled. Someone besides me had used magic. It wasn't Mason. I'd have felt his magic differently.

I looked around the apartment. The tingle began to hurt just a bit. I'd had negative magic focused on me, but not like this. It felt bad to be there.

"Let's go," I said to Mason. "I'll feed you downstairs."

Mason trotted to the door in front of me. I grabbed my purse. I reached the door and turned the knob, which wouldn't move.

I tried again.

Nothing.

I pulled out my key to insert it and see if that made a difference. Nothing.

The hinges are on the inside. You could find a tool and take them off, Mason said helpfully, sensing my worry.

Instead, I sent a magical call for help to the local police department. It was sort of a fail-safe for witches against magical attack. I hoped that the witch who had been in here hadn't come from a witch community. They wouldn't have thought about my ability to call for help telepathically.

I watched as the afghan that my mom had made worked its way off the sofa and slithered towards me, like a snake.

The bedroom, Mason said. *Close the door.*

He leaped around the blanket, which tried to catch him in the act but Mason was fast. He hissed.

I hurried behind him, leaping over the blanket not unlike he did and landing behind him. I hurried into the bedroom, with Mason running in front.

The comforter on my bed raised itself up. I paused, wondering what to do next. I was surrounded by blankets. My mind couldn't quite wrap itself around the situation. I was afraid of a blanket. Killer blankets? It was the sort of spoof on horror movies that Trinity loved to watch and I was smack dab in the middle of it. With magic, even stupid horror movies could end up being true.

Bathroom, Mason said. He wasn't distracted by the ridiculousness of the situation.

The bathroom was right next to the bedroom and Mason leaped inside. I slipped inside and tried to slam the door. The afghan was across the threshold far enough to keep me from being able to do it.

I nudged the blanket with my foot. It wrapped itself around my foot and tried to pull. I squealed and pushed it away as far as I could.

Mason leaped on it, biting at the threads that were trying to climb my leg and wrap itself around me like a giant snake.

Instead, the afghan wrapped itself around Mason's head.

I felt it squeezing my leg and worried for him.

I pulled him back. The afghan remained wrapped around him. I pulled at it with my hands. I was the preferred target and it let go of Mason to wrap around my hands.

Foolish, Mason said. *I could have stopped it from getting to you.*

"You could have died!" I screamed.

Your magic is more powerful than mine, Mason reminded me. I didn't know what kind of spell would work. Once again, I needed a spell to defend myself but had nothing. You'd think I would have learned that last time. I searched through my repertoire of spells and came up empty. I mean, I had found something to distract, but that was distracting another witch. How did you distract a blanket?

I let out a small hysterical laugh because how could I not? I listened for sirens but there were none. I sent out another call, wondering where the police were.

I had protection spells, but not protection from threads and yarn. I had protection from fleas and chanted that.

Nothing.

Fleas? Mason thought at me. He sat back in the bathtub. I felt his energy ready to help when something worked.

Fire would work but I didn't want to take the chance of burning down the building. Of course, I had protections against fire. The familiars downstairs were valuable.

The café was still open. I thumped on the floor, hoping that if the police didn't arrive, Greg or someone would come upstairs wondering what was going on.

Mason picked up on that and sent a message to the familiars in the room. I soon heard yowling and screaming. I hoped that the visitors were witches and not ordinaries. If they were ordinaries, they were probably scared out of their mind. Witches would know something was wrong.

I tried a cleaning spell. Mentally, I imagined the blanket twisting around in an imaginary washer but, of course, cleaning spells just get stains out and the afghan attacking me continued on, crawling up my leg, hoping to hug me to death.

Knocking came from the front door. I hoped whoever it was would just come in, except, not only was the door magically locked, but I'd locked it normally.

It's Greg, Mason said.

I hoped that he'd be eager to play hero and break the door down.

Unfortunately, the knocking stopped and I heard nothing more.

Try a charm spell, Mason suggested. *I'll enhance it and maybe you can charm the blanket off.*

"Blankets can't be charmed," I said. "They don't have intelligence."

They also aren't supposed to be able to slither across the floor and attack someone on their own, Mason pointed out.

By this time the comforter from the bed was also at the door. I had it partially closed so it wasn't like it could completely trap me in there, but each time I tried and failed, the afghan got a little better hold on me.

I tried the charm spell. Then I asked the afghan to leave me alone.

Nothing happened.

"See?" I said.

You didn't think it would work, so of course it didn't, Mason replied easily. *At this point, fire is the best bet. The protection spells should put that out as soon as they notice. You'll have damage in the bathroom but the rest of the place should be okay. I can even help you contain it.*

I started drawing in energy to do a fire spell when I heard the sounds of several people running up the stairs.

My door banged open.

"WBI! Identify yourselves!" a voice that sounded suspiciously like Lina called.

"Jade Owlens! In the bathroom with my familiar Mason. I'm being attacked by an afghan!"

I thought I heard laughter cut off. I listened as my rescuer walked across the floor. The comforter drew back from the doorway.

I heard swearing. Then nothing.

"Hello?" I called. I started drawing in fire energy.

"I'm fine. The damned thing is heavy. And the spell is strong." Lina appeared in the doorway.

She looked at me, the afghan wrapped around one leg and both arms like we were in a deadly game of Twister around the bathroom door.

"Let go." Lina pointed her hand and I felt magic swirling around the room. The afghan resisted and then dropped away.

"I'll need to take both blankets, as they were used in an assault," she said. "There's more than just the negative spell on them. Who did the spells?"

"I did the one on the comforter to make sure I had restful sleep. My mom did the one on the afghan for calming."

Lina didn't even bother to make a note. She cocked her head and looked at me. "I think it's safe to come out of the bathroom unless you were planning on doing something else in there?"

I tried to avoid glaring, but doubted I was successful. Once through the door, I noted two Waverton police officers in the apartment along with a man in plain clothes that I hadn't seen before.

"Gather up the blankets, check everything in the apartment for magical signatures," Lina said.

"My protection spells are really good," I said. "No one should have been able to get in. And it's not like I take the blankets out with me."

I rubbed my arms. I couldn't imagine how anyone had gotten in.

"You have images on your protection spells?" the man asked. He was taking notes.

The Waverton police were the ones gathering things up. An older man came into the apartment and started spraying something in the air. I noticed that it turned purple when it touched the doorknob.

"I don't," I said.

"The spells are strong, though," Lina interrupted me.

The man nodded.

"No one entered," the older man who was spraying whatever it was in the apartment said.

"Distance magic?" Lina asked.

"Probably used a camera to get a visual on what was here. Probably why they used a blanket instead of, say, a piece of jewelry. Harder to see," the man said.

"Still, the protection spell?" Lina asked.

"Got through the wards. Damned powerful. I'd bet that the witch either had help or had a powerful familiar working with them," the man said.

The younger man was still taking notes.

"You and your familiar will need to find somewhere else to sleep tonight," Lina said.

I sighed. At least I had Mason's stuff packed in the car. I started for the bedroom to pack a quick bag.

"Nothing from the apartment goes. Chances are your clothing wasn't in plain sight if that's how the witch cast the spells, but let's not take chances. I don't want to have warnings hitting me from wherever you end up staying. Are there rooms at the hotel?" Lina asked.

"Don't know. I have family here and I'm sure my parents will let me stay with them, seeing I probably can't just go to my sister's." Not that I'd be comfortable at Julia's if she wasn't there.

"Not a crime scene any longer, but I wouldn't recommend it. I'd rather you had people around you," Lina said. "The hotel would be better. Are you sure your friend can't get you a room?"

"If you insist, she probably can, but why not my family?" I asked.

"Harder to pinpoint where you are and what's around in a hotel. The WBI can get a different blanket than what's normally there. Keep the drapes closed, bring in different towels and there's nothing to focus on from a distance. And, as we found when we were investigating there, the hotel has a network of protection spells to attempt to keep crime to a minimum," Lina said.

"Not that it helped," I said. "Because apparently, this witch can slither through protection spells."

"Slither…" the younger man said. "I like that. It's what this feels like." He made another note.

Lina didn't acknowledge his input. "Call your friend."

I went to my phone. No one stopped me from grabbing that. I called Natalie and told her what happened. It took longer than it should have because she had some choice words about me being attacked before I even told her what Lina wanted.

"We just cleaned and sanitized the room where Shannon was when she died," Natalie said.

"They only have Shannon's old room," I said, looking at Lina.

"Find a different one," Lina said. "Someone there must piss her off enough to toss."

"Did you hear?" I asked Natalie.

The laughter told me she had.

"I actually have a room on the top floor next to the owner's suite," Natalie said. "It's a corner room and a little cramped so I almost never put anyone in that room unless we're really booked and someone begs."

"Kind of like me," I said.

"Exactly," Natalie said. "And seeing the WBI is bringing different bedding and towels, they'll be happy to know the bed is only a double. The linens are the old ones we had before the last makeover so the colors are different, although the towels are still white."

"I'll let Lina know. I guess I'm going to go shopping for a toothbrush and some underwear. I'm not allowed to remove anything from the room."

"I have a nightshirt I can loan you," Natalie said. "I'll call Trinity and see if she has some sweats you can wear. You're closer in size."

"Great," I said.

I hung up and looked at Lina.

"See, everything works out," Lina smiled at me in what might have been supposed to be reassuring but wasn't.

I grabbed Mason's carrier, dared someone to tell me I couldn't take that or my purse, and walked out the door.

I fumed all the way to the hotel. I couldn't believe I wasn't even allowed to take a toothbrush. Lina was pretty sure the witch who had put a spell on things hadn't been in my apartment and was using what she could see, but they were worried about a toothbrush? The hotel had them for visitors but I was going to need to go out and get some underwear because there was no way I was borrowing that.

I realized that I'd be judging in whatever clothes I had with me. When I got to the parking lot of the hotel, I called my mom.

"Do you have any of my old clothes there?" I asked.

"I'm sure I do in the big closet in the basement," Mom said.

"There was an incident in my apartment. The afghan that you made me and my comforter tried to murder me and the WBI sent me off and I wasn't allowed to take anything. I mean, I took Mason's carrier and my purse anyway because I needed that stuff to drive, but I don't have any clothing and I have to judge tomorrow and…" I trailed off, near tears.

"I'll find something," Mom said. "I have some old clothes of mine, too, that might fit you. And we're the same shoe size. I have those black flats, would that work?"

They weren't the style I was looking for but they'd look reasonably professional.

"Those would be fine," I said.

"Why don't you just come here?" Mom asked.

"The WBI wants me in a hotel where it will be harder for a witch to try and do negative magic on something inside again. They're even bringing in a different set of towels and blankets."

"You're kidding?! And does Natalie even have room what with the fair and all?"

"She said the small room upstairs next to the owner's suite is open. They don't like to put anyone in there unless they really beg for an extra room. It was either that or Shannon's room which I didn't want and the WBI wasn't thrilled about putting me in," I said. I wiped my nose.

"Did you really say the afghan tried to murder you?" Mom asked suddenly.

"It's kind of stupid, isn't it?" I asked, laughing a little. "I mean, I could have been killed by a blanket."

"But you're okay?" Now Mom was in full-on mama bear mode and I was going to have to reassure her that I was fine. Clearly, it had taken her some time to parse that I said I had nearly been murdered by a blanket.

Not that I blamed her. I had a feeling that was going to be happening a lot.

So we talked a bit longer. Mason started getting restless in the back. He was probably annoyed with my mother's questions and just wanted to get out and wander somewhere, even if it wasn't his house. He did have an unfinished meal. Which reminded me I was going to have to go and get him some of his food.

I finally calmed my mom down and she said she'd be over soon. I asked her to bring food and cat litter and stuff for Mason. I had no idea how long I'd have to stay in the hotel. Then I texted Natalie and told her I was in the parking lot with Mason.

When she responded, I grabbed my purse and Mason and headed in. The other stuff could wait until I could grab a cart and bring it up. Not that I had much other stuff. Just odds and ends for Mason to get settled in the kennel at the fair.

Natalie met me at the door and hugged me. She gave me the key and insisted on helping me take Mason upstairs.

"I can't believe you almost died," she said.

"But I didn't," I replied.

"Who could have done it? Did you see anyone?" she asked.

I shook my head. "And I don't know why they'd go after me. I did ask some questions, but like I told Tyson, no more than, say, Deena. And Ben's even a suspect."

"Maybe because you're related to Julia?" Natalie said. "Or maybe they think you know something that you don't."

"I wish I did know whatever it is they think I know. At least then I could tell the WBI." I went back to feeling a little sorry for myself. Tyson wasn't pleased with me because he thought I was asking too many questions for my own good. Now, he could say he told me so. Except I hadn't asked that many questions.

I'd been wandering around the fair and listening to people.

When we got in the elevator, Natalie looked at me and asked, "How does someone almost get killed by a blanket?"

I rolled my eyes and explained what had happened.

"And you know what?" I said. "I'm kind of mad. I mean I love that afghan—Mom made it for me—but how can I ever enjoy sitting under it again when it tried to kill me?"

"Are you sure it wanted to kill you?" Natalie asked.

"It floated off the sofa and came towards me. When Mason leaped on it to try and keep it from getting inside the bathroom, squeezed him around the head. Yes, I'm pretty sure it was trying to kill me. The comforter probably would have just worked on smothering, but the afghan stitching is too loose for that so it had to work on squeezing or strangling."

Natalie sighed. The bell dinged when we reached the top floor. There were ordinary rooms up there as well as the owner's suite and the smaller corner room they tried not to use.

The hall smelled of hotel smells, as always, but also strongly of pizza. I wondered if whoever had the owner's suite was having a party.

The room door was off the main hall on a short passage. Natalie opened it for me, turning on a light and then allowing me to go ahead of her. While it was smaller than the other rooms, it wasn't bad. The space across from the closet would make a good corner for the litter box. The bathroom was basic and without a tub but I wasn't planning on staying long enough to miss a tub. At least I hoped I wouldn't.

The main part of the room was smaller than usual. The bed wasn't done in the usual white with a blue sash. This one had a cream and beige comforter, no sash at all. The single chair in the corner was worn green rather than gray or blue.

"The WBI called and said they'd be delivering brightly colored towels. You're not to open the drapes and I made sure they were closed the minute you called to ask about a room."

"I guess that leaves toilet paper," I said. Although that was typically so thin it would be tough to find a way to use it as an instrument of death.

Natalie walked further into the room and set Mason's carrier down. I opened it so he could nose around. His ears weren't straight up so he was not pleased with his treatment. I rubbed his head.

I dislike the smell in here. Too antiseptic. And it's small, he complained.

We won't be here long, I thought back at him. I didn't want Natalie to know my cat didn't approve of the room she'd given us.

"I called my mom," I told her. "She'll be coming by with clothes and some shoes for tomorrow."

"That's right! Tomorrow is your competition!" Natalie put a hand to her face. "I should have had someone get you something."

"Don't worry about it. Mom was going to look through some of her older clothes and we'll find something that will fit," I said. Mom was normally a bit larger than I was, especially in the chest but she did keep some of her "thin" clothing that would fit me. The tops might be a bit large but I could always belt it and make the look work.

Natalie flopped onto the chair and looked at me.

"Who do you think did this?"

"I have no clue," I said. "I haven't talked to anyone today except maybe Deena. I did briefly talk to Lyn Upton but I can't see her as the murderer."

"Lyn was always a little jealous of you working with animals you know. She loved them, but she got married so early that she didn't finish more than a year of college," Natalie said.

"But to kill me?" I asked.

Natalie shrugged.

"Anyone here who seems suspicious?" I asked.

"Everyone here is suspicious, if you ask me. I have several

of the working cat folks from out of town. Clay Spencer is definitely weird. He takes all his food upstairs and eats with his familiar. He swears the cat won't eat if he's not eating with him," Natalie said holding up a finger.

"There's an older woman name Monica Devore. She's in the luxury feline class, but there's best of show which includes all classes, and she demanded two extra sets of towels because she needed one just for her cat. The cat's not even a longhair!" Natalie held up two fingers. "I heard, though, that she didn't place and she's not a happy camper."

I shrugged. I had a feeling that whoever was murdering people was closer to Luanne than someone trying to win best in show. Of course, the favorites were always those from the working classes.

"Shannon was a bit weird because I only saw her leave her room once this whole time. I guess that's not weird, just a little unusual. She could have left when I wasn't around," Natalie said holding up a third finger.

"Maybe she was hiding from someone?" I asked.

"Maybe. I heard that her breakup with Ben was messy. I've been listening to gossip about them since you told me they dated."

I nodded.

"Of course, a couple of other women were talking about her and I don't think they liked her. Oh! The woman with the dog with the weird name, Celia!" Natalie said.

"I've run into her a couple of times with her group of friends. She seems really negative," I said.

"I liked her when we talked, but she's complained about several things. She's staying in a room with a mousy woman who doesn't say much."

"Could it be one of them?" I asked.

"Well, Celia has a dog in the working group," Natalie said.

"And I think it was favored," I added thinking back.

"But why Shannon?" Natalie asked. "That doesn't make sense. From what I understand Celia and her friends aren't part of the craft group."

"You said you liked Celia," I said.

"I said she seemed nice," Natalie said. "I'm inclined to trust her but…"

"So we keep her on the list," I finished.

Natalie nodded quickly before continuing. "There's Olivia still, and she has the better motive."

"It's hard to picture her killing her cousin," I said. "I mean, I have a hard time picturing her killing anyone, but especially her cousin."

"And you said Lyn Upton acted weird to you, so I'd put her on the list. Her brother's wife is entered in the quilt show, so she'd have reason to kill both women."

"Seems thin to me," I said. I hated to think I went to school with someone who could be a murderer.

"But she's the only one with a personal reason to go after you," Natalie protested.

"I don't see it," I said. "It's a silly reason to think about killing someone."

Natalie sighed. Her phone buzzed with a text. She was already responding before the buzzing stopped.

"I have to go. We're still getting complaints about the police and the WBI which my dad is letting me handle. Gee thanks, Dad!" Natalie stood up, waved, and headed out.

When she left, Mason leaped up on the bed next to me.

It still stinks in here. And did you get dinner? He asked.

"Mom's coming with it," I said. "You'll live."

Barely. It hardly seems fair to live through the attack of the afghan only to starve to death an hour later.

"Hopefully, Mom will hurry," I said rubbing his ears. After not having an appetite all day, I was suddenly nearly as hungry as the cat. It must have been the fact that I was finally starting to relax after the terror of almost being killed.

I considered going out to find something to eat but decided it would be safer to use room service. At least I hoped it was. Even so, I had to eat every bit as much as Mason did.

24

The next morning I drove with Mason and all his cat stuff to the fair. Mom had come by after driving out of town to one of the dollar shops to get new underwear for me. I guess no one in town had any. Which reminded me how much I rely on online shopping and the time and ability to drive into London or Louisville.

Mason had plenty of cat food for however long we had to stay, and Mom even brought cat treats. I might even go so far as to say he was grateful for the cat treats, which meant he basically stopped complaining so much about not getting food once he'd been served treats and his regular dinner.

Tyson came by with dinner for the two of us, which we ate picnic-style in the room. He'd been worried about me and was worried I was in trouble for asking questions. He wanted me to promise I'd stop. I reminded him I wasn't even asking that many questions. Mostly I was just listening to people. He wasn't happy with me, but at least he gave me a kiss when he left.

In the morning I dressed in my borrowed clothing. Mom's shoes fit. They weren't really my style, but most of her shoes were high-heeled pumps that I'd probably break an ankle trying to wear. I prefer something a bit lower than two or three inches. I had no idea what had prompted her to buy a pair of ballet flats.

The initial dress she brought was a little tight across my hips. The next two were a bit too big, however, one would look nice with a belt, which she had packed up, just in case. With the belt, the dress looked like a blousy blue t-shirt dress that hung just below my knees. Mom wanted to bunch it up so that it came just above the knee where it hit her, but I liked the longer length.

In the morning, when she was gone, I added a pair of leggings that Trinity had dropped by after Mom had left. I was going to be bending and stooping and working with cats. I needed to look nice but I also needed to be confident that my butt wasn't going to hang out if I had to chase down a recalcitrant familiar. Most familiars would stick by their witch, but now and then one would decide that running around and making the judges chase them was far more fun than being a good familiar.

Saturday traffic was lighter. I was early enough that the crowds weren't even forming at the gates. It looked like luck might be on my side and I made it easily to the judge's parking lot.

I grabbed Mason and his stuff, which I was getting thoroughly tired of hauling around, and headed into the fairgrounds. The day was cloudy and cool, but I'd heard it was supposed to clear up in the afternoon and no rain was forecast. I smelled the fresh sawdust that had been laid down overnight to make sure that everything stayed cleaner. I noticed the small ruts that had formed when it rained had been completely smoothed out, too.

The competition building was noisier than it usually was. The working feline class wasin a few hours. The working equine group began at nine. I suspected those judges were already in the building. Other judges were around. Different ones.

Of course, there would be all class competitions starting in the afternoon. The canine working class judges were all there hashing something out. They were early, but I had noticed they hadn't been around much for the last couple of days.

A dog barked once when I went past. Mason shifted his weight.

Finally, I reached the office we'd been using. Ben was already there, working on the computer.

"Morning," I said.

"I heard you had an eventful evening," he said, looking up. Night Shadow stretched and came over to the edge of the kennel. I wasn't sure if she was greeting me or Mason.

Picking up Mason to put him in his kennel I got the answer.

Me, of course.

Naturally. I wouldn't rate a feline greeting.

"Unfortunately," I said in response to Ben's comment.

"I don't understand who would want to murder you," Ben said.

Deena bustled in with Bistro just then. She shook her head as Ben spoke. "I heard about that. I can't believe you were in such danger and didn't call me!"

"I called my mom," I said. "And my friend Natalie had things set up for me at the hotel."

"You didn't have to stay in Shannon's old room, did you? I heard they were full up," Deena went on.

I shook my head. "There's a small room in a corner that they don't usually rent out unless it's an emergency. I guess I qualified."

Deena gave a nod. "Well, that's good." She looked me up

and down. Ben was in a nice suit, the jacket hanging over the chair. Deena was in an equally nice pantsuit in beige with a bright purple blouse.

"I heard they didn't let you take anything from your apartment," Deena said. "Did you find that outfit in town?"

"Sort of," I said. "My friend Trinity brought over some leggings. My mom had the dress but it was a little big."

Deena nodded. "You did good, then. I'll make a note of it for LaDona. Are you sure you're set for the judging?"

"I think it will take my mind off things," I told her.

I knelt down near Mason. I needed to get him some water. I could do that in a minute. He bumped his head against my hand.

I smell something, he said. *It reminds me of the apartment last night.*

Be ready, I told him. No way was I speaking out loud. Only Ben and Deena were in the room, but both seemed to know more about the attack than I would have expected. I wondered which of them might have done it. Ben had been so kind. Intellectual, but kind. He'd been in the hotel when Shannon had been killed. And his room was near hers.

Deena hadn't been staying there, but I had no idea where she was staying. She'd managed to get to the competition the next day. I bit my tongue to keep from asking her where she stayed. Of course, she seemed to know everyone so maybe someone had a room in town. I should have checked. But, she was warm and kind and seemed like the last person who would murder someone.

I stood up, pulling magic in, wishing I had time to take some defensive magic classes. I'd thought that the one time I'd needed it would be the only time. It's not like witches get into magical duals or murders all the time. I knew some basic ordinary self-defense and normally that and a protection spell were all I'd ever need.

Deena had placed a long thin fleece scarf on the chair. I watched as the end wiggled a bit. The hairs on my neck rose. My arms tingled. Magic.

Ben frowned.

"The scarf!" he choked out, looking at it.

Deena was on the floor with Bistro. She leaned back, looking at the scarf that paused near her, like a cobra about to strike.

"What?!" Deena said. "What's going on?!"

I slipped by both of them, planning to look out into the hallway. Deena had her scarf with her most of the time. Negative magic required that at some point someone have at least seen the object, though touching was preferable. Given that Deena hadn't been targeted earlier, I suspect the user wasn't far.

I reached the door but it slammed in my face. Other people were banging on their doors.

I stepped back. The WBI had to know something was going on. This had to have triggered every alarm they had as well as all the alarms the Waverton police had, not to mention the fair security.

While I had my back to it, the scarf had stopped menacing Deena and was facing me. It leaped towards my neck. I put my hands up and caught the thing.

I felt it moving. The whole thing felt slimy, like a snake, but I held it away.

Deena chanted something under her breath. I worried that it was negative magic, strengthening it to try and strangle me. I didn't want to believe I had misjudged someone that badly.

Instead of negative tingles, I felt calm coming over me. The scarf dropped.

Ben breathed out.

"What's going on?" he asked. "Who would want to harm

all of us?"

Deena shook her head. She looked pale, drawn, as if the magic had sapped her. I wondered if it was the calming magic or if she'd been the one to set the negative spell. I felt pretty sure Ben wasn't involved.

The door swung open. The woman I kept seeing around the fair strode in, her short red hair looking slightly mussed. She had a small dog with her, a beagle from the look of his black and tan fur and stance.

She frowned at Deena. Then looked at me. And sighed.

"You interfering bitch. I should have taken care of you when I took care of Shannon," she said.

Then she pointed a finger at me.

I felt the negative magic pour through the room, my arms and legs tingling with energy. It felt every bit as slimy as the scarf. I struggled to breathe.

I had a moment of clarity when I noticed that both Deena and Ben were also struggling to breathe.

"Why?" I managed.

Celia tilted her head back a bit.

I noticed Night Shadow looking as if she were also struggling. Which meant Mason was as well.

Fury rode through my body. I might give in if she were trying to kill me, but not my familiar.

"You kept following me around. You were going to find out what Shannon saw sooner or later!" Celia snapped.

The beagle barked once.

I reached out telepathically to Mason. I couldn't quite reach him but I felt his magic flowing to me. I used the only protection spell I had and pushed the magic out and around the room. I didn't know how to stop Celia's magic, but if I could make a big enough bubble then we could all breathe. Maybe I could even force the negative spell back on Celia.

I managed a breath. I kept pushing. Mason was fading

and I pushed the bubble of air out further. I felt him start to pant. Relief flooded through me.

I didn't have to hold this long. Just long enough for the WBI to get there. Just long enough for someone to break down any other barriers that Celia might have put up.

Ben gasped for air. He pulled Night Shadow's kennel into the circle. Then he grabbed Deena who looked near to fainting. Finally, he pulled Bistro closer.

I felt him add his strength to mine, pushing the bubble further outwards towards Celia.

Deena sat on the floor holding her head.

"You've been on the circuit long enough," Deena panted. "What were you thinking? Why?"

"Gossip you missed?" Celia asked, glaring at Deena. I noticed Celia's face was puffy and red. We were beating her. The beagle was looking worn down, just a bit. His tail was no longer up and he pranced in place a few times, struggling.

"Apparently," Deena agreed.

Ben did something to strengthen the bubble around us. It felt as if he'd placed the end of a heavy object on something so we weren't holding it ourselves. I'd have to ask him what he did when we were done. For the moment I wanted to hear what Celia had to say.

Just as suddenly, Celia dropped her magic.

I almost fell forward, I was so intent upon extending the protection bubble.

Then something hard slammed into me. Not Celia. Just a focus of magic. The protection bubble was still around me, so the slam was hard but not lethal.

Ben staggered a moment.

"What did I miss?" Deena asked.

"Luanne was going to report me for dating one of the judges and not disclosing," Celia snapped. "And then Shannon saw us together. I had a lock on this competition!"

"Your final one," Deena said. "Why not disclose and wait?"

The beagle whined again.

"Kandy Karmen's got cancer," Celia said. "We wouldn't have finished together! And then that bitch Luanne laughed about keeping me from getting that final win!"

Celia even shed a few tears then.

Deena stood up and chanted something. I felt the pressure from whatever had slammed into me loosen.

Then she went and hugged Celia as tightly as she could. I let my jaw drop to my chin. Ben patted me on the shoulder for a moment, a thin smile. Then he looked up and nodded at the door.

Lina stood there, three other WBI officers with her. They looked as if they'd been through the wringer.

L ina directed the WBI agents to take Celia into custody. She stayed with us to get our statements. If they'd been listening, Celia had basically confessed to the murders.

"She said that Luanne was going to report her for being involved with one of the judges," I said.

"Probably Joe Landry," Ben said quietly.

Deena nodded. "I'd heard he had something going on that he didn't want to talk about."

"He could have canceled on the show," Ben said.

"He's got about five black marks for canceling at the last minute already," Deena added.

Lina watched each of them, a slight smile playing about her lips.

I wanted to ask her what was up.

I was sitting down near Mason's kennel. He was out on my lap, keeping tabs on things. His fur felt a little too soft. He'd worked and been overstressed but I knew he'd be fine.

Night Shadow sat on Ben's desk, a paw on his arm. Bistro

laid in the chair in front of where Deena had knelt down after getting him out of his kennel.

Someone came in as we were each telling our stories and reminded us that we had a competition to judge. Lina started to say something but Deena cut her off. Apparently, the competition must go on.

Instead of taking our familiars in carriers, each of us made the decision to carry ours out to the floor. The room felt huge to me after being in the small office with multiple other people. Lina waited at the door, watching.

I got through it, somehow. Mason made minimal sarcastic comments about it being easier to work when he could breathe. Ben and Deena moved through the judging by rote. I tried to keep a smile, but had no idea if I succeeded.

Eventually, the competition was over and I carried Mason back to the office. Lina joined us as I was packing up Mason's items.

"I have a few more questions," she said.

I groaned.

Deena smiled and hugged me. I felt magic tingling along my arms. I wanted to melt into her. My legs could barely hold me up, I felt so relaxed.

Ben looked over at us. "That's what she was doing to Celia. No one can withstand Deena's magic hug."

Lina raised an eyebrow. When Deena let me go, I sighed and slumped into my chair. I felt like I'd enjoyed an hour-long massage and just needed a nap.

"Will Julia be set free?" I asked.

Lina gave a single nod. Good.

Then she took us through the events one more time. I tried not to roll my eyes. She'd been around for much of it. I'd learned, for instance, that Celia had magically barricaded the doors to the outside as well as individual judges' rooms.

She'd also set up some booby traps along the hallway, which was why Lina had looked a bit worn out when she got there.

I suspected that magic was why Celia hadn't been able to hold onto her magic in our room, and probably why it was so easy for Deena to defeat the scarf.

Finally, the interrogation was over and I could take Mason and be off. Unfortunately, given the traps that had been set in the hallway, Lina wasn't going to allow me back to my apartment because they hadn't quite finished checking everything. They hadn't found anything else spelled, at least not yet, but they were taking no chances.

While we'd been talking LaDona bustled in. She looked at each of us in turn. "I don't have to tell you that this was a scandal but you three handled it as well as could be expected. At least the competition wasn't delayed. That would have been a disaster!" LaDona glared at Lina, probably for even suggesting such a thing.

"Jade was amazing," Deena said. "I can't wait to work with her again!"

LaDona pursed her lips at first. Deena held her gaze with such force, I thought she was willing LaDona to keep me on the judging roster.

"I suppose she did handle herself well enough in an unusual circumstance," LaDona finally said. Then she turned to me. "I'll be keeping you on the roster to see how you do in an ordinary competition. The board would have my head if I went against Deena's recommendation."

Once LaDona had left, I looked forward to heading to the hotel and ordering up some room service. Knowing Julia was out of jail, or soon would be, gave me an appetite. Plus, using magic always made me hungry. I was surprised the three of us had made it through the competition without a snack. I'd been eyeing the cat treats longingly even as I fed extras to Mason while Deena and Ben had fed their familiars.

I stopped at a drive-thru on the way to the hotel. I sat in the parking lot and ate so I could feed Mason some of my food. It wasn't good for him, but we both needed the calories.

The sun was out and the sky was blue and the day was a good one.

My phone rang as I was eating.

Tyson.

"Hello?" I said.

"I heard you were almost killed again this morning," he said.

"It was Celia. And the stupid thing was, it wasn't that I was asking so many questions. It was that she thought I was following her because I kept running into her when I was wandering around the fair!" I said. The one time I hadn't seen her was when I actually was asking questions. So much for his theory.

"I heard who it was," Tyson said. "I just helped Julia get processed out of jail. Tom took her home."

"I'm glad to hear it," I said.

"Are you back home yet?"

I explained the WBI's worries.

"I'm glad they're being thorough. I wouldn't want you to go home and find something else attacking you."

"Because you know, there's probably a stupider way to die than being attacked by a blanket," I said.

"Don't laugh. It might not be a typical way to die, but you'd still be dead. And I'd be the one to have to pick up pieces," Tyson said. "Want to picnic in your room again or are you allowed into the restaurant near the hotel."

"I think that I can go anywhere, but I did have to do some heavy magic this morning," I said. "Mason and I are having a fast food snack on the way to the hotel."

"I'll give you an hour then and pick you. We'll go to the

restaurant that's there. Nothing fancy but you can order all you want," Tyson said.

"I'll be there with an appetite, I'm sure."

"Jade," Tyson said, "You know I worry about you, right? I don't want to fight with you about what you do, but I can't help but want to try and protect you. I hate that you were targeted by a murderer."

"I know," I said.

"If something happened to you, I don't know what I'd do," Tyson said. "It seems like we're both so busy that we never really have much time together. I think we need to work on that."

"Let's talk at dinner. When I've had enough food to come up with creative ideas, okay?"

"It's a date."

And with that, he rang off.

I looked at Mason pleased.

At least last time you two had a heart to heart I only had to pretend to nearly die, Mason said, scarfing down a French fry.

"I was working on saving you," I said.

I feel weak from oxygen deprivation and the use of magic, Mason replied. *I will be getting more dinner, won't I?*

"Of course you will," I said.

Mason washed a paw and said nothing. Of course not. More dinner was clearly his due. We finished our quick snack and headed back to the hotel. I was looking forward to dinner with Tyson and then relaxing in the room with Mason.

Of course, that didn't happen because I had to talk to Natalie and Trinity, and by the time Tyson got me out of there I was about to fight Mason for another can of cat food. But finally, my growling stomach freed me from their questions so I could eat my own dinner.

Which led to heading back to the hotel and other things

that Mason, fortunately, was too sleepy to comment on. And it seemed like Tyson and I were both committed to spending more time together no matter what else was going on in our lives, which made me smile, eager to see where our relationship took us.

Bonnie Elizabeth could never decide what to do, so she wrote stories about amazing things and sometimes she even finished them.

While rejection stung her so badly in person, she spent most of her young life talking to cats and dogs rather than people, she was unusually resilient when it came to rejections on her writing, racking up a good number of them.

Floating through a variety of jobs, including veterinary receptionist, cemetery administrator, and finally acupuncturist, she continued to write stories.

When the internet came along (yes she's old), she started blogging as her cat, because we all know cats don't notice rejection. Then she started publishing.

Bonnie writes in a variety of genres. Her popular Whisper series is contemporary fantasy and her Teenage Fairy Godmother series is written for teens. She has been published in a number of anthologies and is working on expanding her writing repertoire.

She lives with her husband (who talks less than she does) and her three cats, who always talk back.

Stay in Touch

Little Dog Lost

Death Interrupted

Down in Whisper

A Haunting Whisper

A Haunting Attraction

Secrets Not Whispers

Only Human

OTHER NOVELS

One Bad Wish

Sun Spot Magic

Ghosts from the Past

Unnatural Secrets

Shadows of Solstice

The Haunting of Steely Woods

Find them all at your favorite bookseller or check us out at
MyBigFatOrangeCat.com